What [...]
Charism[...]
A body to die f[...] [...]he
crowd. Well, [...] [...]ew
collection has s[...] all this—and more!
And now that they've met the women in these
novels, there is one thing on everyone's mind....

NIGHTS OF PASSION

One night is never enough!

The guys know what they want and how they're
going to get it!

Don't miss any of these hot stories
this month in Modern Love!

The Tycoon's Virgin
Susan Stephens

Bedded for Diamonds
Kelly Hunter

His for the Taking
Julie Cohen

Purchased for Pleasure
Nicola Marsh

We'd love to hear what you think
about any of these books.
Email us at Presents@hmb.co.uk or find out more
information at www.iheartpresents.com

Accidentally educated in the sciences, **KELLY HUNTER** has always had a weakness for fairy tales, fantasy worlds and losing herself in a good book. Husband...yes. Children...two boys. Cooking and cleaning...sigh. Sports...no, not really—in spite of the best efforts of her family. Gardening...yes—roses, of course. Kelly was born in Australia and has traveled extensively. Although she enjoys living and working in different parts of the world, she still calls Australia home.

Kelly Hunter

Bedded for Diamonds

HARLEQUIN®

TORONTO • NEW YORK • LONDON
AMSTERDAM • PARIS • SYDNEY • HAMBURG
STOCKHOLM • ATHENS • TOKYO • MILAN • MADRID
PRAGUE • WARSAW • BUDAPEST • AUCKLAND

ISBN-13: 978-0-373-82090-0
ISBN-10: 0-373-82090-9

BEDDED FOR DIAMONDS

First North American Publication 2008.

Previously published in the U.K. under the title PRICELESS.

Copyright © 2006 by Kelly Hunter.

www.eHarlequin.com

Printed in U.S.A.

Bedded for Diamonds

CHAPTER ONE

ERIN SINCLAIR WAS used to traffic. Rush hour traffic, gridlocked traffic, rainy-day traffic…and, right now, airport traffic. Sydney was a vibrant, picturesque city with an iconic bridge and a bluer than blue harbour, but Sydney roads at eight a.m. on a Monday morning were congested.

Taxi drivers knew these things.

Her passengers had been running late, but she'd delivered them to the international departure terminal in record time thanks to a run of green lights. They'd tipped big, too rushed to wait for change. Probably not the best start to their day, thought Erin, but it was certainly an excellent way to start hers. Now all she needed was a fare back into the city.

Her pick-up area, the one for luxury taxis, was directly outside the arrival terminal doors. There were no other taxis and no one was waiting for a ride but that didn't stop her from sliding the car to a halt, popping the boot, and getting out. She wouldn't have to wait long.

As requested, she was wearing black. Black hiking

boots, semi-regulation black trousers, black T-shirt. A perky black chauffeur's cap sat ignored on the front passenger seat.

The man who came striding through the arrival terminal doors was not wearing black but, boy, he would have looked good in it. He'd opted instead for scuffed steel-capped boots, green cargo trousers and a grey T-shirt, but that was where Mr Average ended and the fantasy began because the body beneath the everyday clothing was superb.

He was broad-shouldered, slim-hipped, everything about him lean and powerfully muscled. His hair was black and carelessly cut and his face was as near to perfection as the gods would allow. He looked tired. Tired in a way that had nothing to do with a long haul flight and everything to do with a weariness that went soul deep. He was all shut down, which was probably just as well. Because heaven help womankind if he smiled.

He glanced around and started towards her so she headed for the back of the car and pushed the boot open with her fingertips. He was beside her now, and up close she could see that his eyes were the colour of toffee and more than a match for the rest of him. She shot him a smile, reached for his bulky canvas carryall.

'I'll do it.' His voice was deep and quiet.

'Is this a gender thing?'

'I prefer to think of it as a weight thing.' The look he sent her might have been swift, but what it lacked in longevity it made up for in intensity. She felt the force of it, of him, clear through to her soul. 'You're not very big, are you?' he said finally.

Erin blew out the breath she hadn't realised she'd been holding and pushed a wayward strand of short brown hair from her eyes. So she was five feet four and a little on the slender side. This wasn't news. Maybe he hadn't seen clear through to her soul after all. If he had he'd have known better than to comment on her size.

By the time he'd shut the boot on his luggage she had the passenger door open and was waiting for him to get in. He looked at her, looked at the door, and the faintest of smiles crossed his lips. Obviously he wasn't used to having car doors opened for him either. 'Are you sure you're after a *luxury* taxi service?' she asked him dryly. 'Because the regular taxis are just over there.'

He glanced at the long line of regular taxis, glanced back at her. 'Will a luxury ride get me into the city any faster?'

'Only in your imagination.'

His smile widened fractionally.

'On the upside, I have three different newspapers you can read on the way and I can order in coffee.'

'Good coffee?' he asked.

'Exceptional coffee.'

'Espresso, black, two sugars,' he said, and got in. Men were so easy.

She shut his door and headed for the driver's seat. 'Where to?'

'Albany Street, Double Bay.'

Nice. She picked up her mobile, called in his coffee order, pulled out into the traffic, and set about making his journey a luxury one. 'Newspaper?' she asked. 'I

have the *Sydney Morning Herald*, *The Australian*, or the
Financial Review.'

'No.'

'Music?' There was something for everyone.

'No.'

O-kay. He didn't look as if he wanted conversation
either but she gave it a whirl, just in case. 'So where'd
you fly in from?'

'London.'

'Been away long?' His accent told her he was
Australian.

'Six years.'

'Six years in London? Without a break? No wonder
you look tired.'

'Maybe I will have that paper,' he said, his gaze
meeting hers in the rear vision mirror.

'That would be a "no" to conversation, then?'

'Right.'

She handed him the *Sydney Morning Herald* in
silence. Maybe he was an elite athlete. A soccer player
returning home at the end of the European season after
his team's final crushing defeat. Maybe he'd missed the
winning penalty goal and was barely able to talk through
the weight of his despair. Yeah, that would work. 'You're
not a soccer player, are you?'

'No.'

'A poet?' That would work too. Because he could
have taught Byron himself a thing or two about looking
sexy, unreachable, and sorely in need of comfort all at
the same time.

'No.' He opened the paper. Rattled it.

Fine. Maybe she should forget about her taciturn passenger and concentrate on her driving. She could do that. No problem.

Five minutes later she pulled up outside Café Siciliano, lowered the rear window, and a curvaceous young waitress handed her passenger an espresso in a take-away cup along with two straws of sugar. 'The sugar's already in it,' the girl said. 'This is extra, just in case.'

'You're an angel,' he said in that soft, deep voice and the girl blinked and blushed prettily.

Harrumph! Erin jabbed at the controls and watched as the tinted window slid smoothly closed. He hadn't called *her* an angel for seeing to it that he got coffee in the first place. Ungrateful sod. Her gaze clashed with his in the rear vision mirror and she could have sworn she saw laughter flicker in their depths.

'Pixies can't be angels,' he said solemnly. 'Different fantasy altogether.'

'Gee,' she said. 'Glad we've cleared that up.' He had such glorious eyes. Such a heart-stopping face. She pulled out onto the road a little more abruptly than usual. Forget service with a smile. It was time to deliver the man to his destination.

And then the engine coughed. Not good. It coughed some more as she swung the car around the nearest corner and into a side street and then, with a well-bred splutter, the late-model luxury Mercedes died altogether.

'We seem to have stopped,' he said.

Oh, *now* he wanted to talk. 'Drink your coffee,' she said, and tried to start the car. The ignition turned over but the engine spluttered like an old maid choking on hot tea.

'Could be a fuel problem,' he offered.

'Could be lots of things.' Erin drummed her fingers on the steering wheel and considered her options. First things first. 'I need to get you another ride.'

'No, you don't,' he said. 'You need to pop the hood so we can take a look at what's wrong.'

'You're a mechanic?'

'No, but I know cars.'

'That's close enough.' Erin liked cars. She enjoyed driving them. But she didn't know a whole lot about fixing them. She released the bonnet, got out of the car, and joined him in staring down at the immaculately clean engine. 'What can you do without tools?'

'Check fuses and connections,' he said and set about doing so with a confidence she found reassuring. He had nice hands, hands that looked as if they knew both strength and gentleness. She looked for a ring, a wrist-watch, but he wore no jewellery of any kind. Some things simply didn't need embellishment.

'And I thought chivalry was dead.' There wasn't much she could do to help except stay out of his light so she leaned back against the grille and waited. 'Rescue people often? You're not a firefighter, are you? Emergency services?'

'Do you always measure a man by his occupation?' he asked absently, his attention still on the engine.

'Not always. Sometimes I measure him by his sweet words and pretty face, but that doesn't always work out.'

'I can imagine.'

'Of course, there's always star signs,' she said thoughtfully.

'You mean you judge a person by his *birthday*?' She had his attention now; his complete and utterly incredulous attention.

'Hey, the measurement of man is a tough one. A girl needs all the help she can get.'

'Yes, but *astrology*?'

'I'm thinking Scorpio for you. Moody, intense…' Unbelievable in bed. The mere thought of which was making her fidget. 'But I could be wrong.'

'I suspect you often are.'

He hadn't, she noted, come right out and told her she was wrong. That was interesting. 'You *are* a Scorpio, aren't you? I knew it.'

He regarded her with exasperation. 'It means nothing.'

'Nope, it means that without any more information whatsoever I can start to measure the man. At least, that's the theory.' And after a moment, 'We're quite compatible.'

'Hard to believe,' he murmured dryly.

Erin suppressed a chuckle. 'Yep, with that pretty face it's a good thing you're low on sweet talk otherwise I might be lost.'

His smile was slow in coming but when it arrived it scrambled her brain. 'I try to save the sweet talk,' he said.

'What on earth for?'

'Later.'

Oh, boy. 'I can see how that could work,' she said breathlessly. He should be carrying a sign, she decided. One that said 'Danger! Engage at own risk'. It would be a service to womankind, a necessity really, because if he ever did decide to go after a woman in earnest she'd probably melt. Already there was heat in her cheeks and a fire in the pit of her stomach as a result of that lazy smile and he wasn't even trying. Not really.

'You've got a blown fuel injection fuse.'

Make that not at all. 'I have?'

'Good thing there's a spare.'

'Yeah.' He leaned over to replace it and there was nothing for it but to watch him some more and try not to lose her breath all over again.

'You can try starting the car now.'

'Oh. Right,' she said, and headed for the driver's seat. The car started at once, purring like a well-fed kitten. 'It works.'

'Try not to sound so surprised.' He lowered the bonnet.

'I'm not surprised. I'm grateful. Really.' And after a pause, 'Is it going to happen again?'

'Hard to say,' he said as he got back in the back seat.

So much for a definitive answer. The easiest solution was to drive the car and see. If it stopped again she'd call it in. Meanwhile, Mr International Man of Mystery wanted to go to Double Bay.

With a swift U-turn and a quick corner they slipped seamlessly back into the Sydney morning traffic.

The pixie chauffeur was right. Six years was a long time to be away from home, Tristan Bennett thought as he downed the last of his lukewarm but surprisingly good coffee. He'd settled into London easily enough; he had his work and his apartment, and his sister was over there too now, but there was no denying that it had never really felt like home. He'd gone to London because of his work, travelled all over Europe because of it, but somewhere along the way youthful enthusiasm had given way to weary cynicism and an increasing sense of futility. The fire was gone, the blade had dulled. And then there'd been that last investigation, the horrors of which had left him tired and hurting and wondering if he had it in him to go back for more.

It had been Hallie, his sister, who'd suggested he take some long overdue leave and head back to Australia for a while. Heartland, she told him. The perfect place to fight demons and find peace. The only place.

So here he was. Haunted by nightmares he couldn't shake and fairly sure he was asking too much of the old house that held its own share of memories, both sweet and painful.

'It's this one on the right,' he said as they drew level with the old two-storey weatherboard with its wrap-around verandah, and the pixie nodded as she pulled smoothly into the driveway and cut the engine.

'Is anyone expecting you?' she said with a frown.

'No.' His father was on sabbatical in Greece, his siblings were scattered across the globe, but it didn't matter. They didn't need to be here for him to feel their presence. He was home.

'I know of a good cleaning service if you need one,' she said.

Okay, so the house was a little neglected and the garden was overgrown. Nothing he couldn't fix. 'I can clean,' he said. It wasn't as if he was going to have much else to do.

'You have no idea what those words do to a woman,

do you?' she said as she turned towards him, and he felt the impact of a pair of lively brown eyes and a smile that promised equal measures of passion and laughter. 'I swear it's better than foreplay. If you can cook I'm yours. You're not a chef are you?'

'There you go again,' he said. 'Focussing on what a man does, rather than what he is.'

'Isn't it the same thing?'

'No. And I'm not a chef.'

Her expression was one of mingled relief and disappointment. 'Probably a good thing,' she muttered.

'Probably,' he said, unable to stop his lips from curving, just a little bit.

She wasn't his type. Not that he could say he had a type exactly, just that she wasn't it. She'd surprised him, that was all. When the car had stopped he hadn't expected her first thought to be about how best to get him to his destination. It suggested a generosity of spirit and a focus on others that was uncommon. And then she'd blindsided him with her smart mouth and easy smile, battering away at his defences with the force of butterfly wings and the impact of an armoured tank and before he knew it he was aware of her in a way that was truly disquieting.

His body wanted to know why she wasn't his type. His body seemed to think that she was.

His *body* had spent the last twenty-two hours trapped in a flying tin can and would have normally been at rest right now. He was prepared to allow it a little leeway. 'How much do I owe you?'

'No charge. You fixed the car.'

'I replaced a fuse,' he corrected. 'It's a thirty-minute drive. I have to pay you something.'

'Nope. I've got it covered.' There was a phone ringing somewhere in the car and by the look on her face she badly wanted to answer it. 'Do you mind if I take this call?' she asked on the sixth ring. 'My brother's been trying to contact me all morning and I keep missing him.'

'Go ahead.'

She shot him a quick smile, found the phone. 'Hello?'

'Erin, it's Rory.'

Finally. Erin popped the boot so that her passenger could unload and stepped from the car to give him a hand. Not that he wanted it. 'What's up?'

'It's about the gem-buying trip next week. I'm going to have to bail.'

'What?' Her voice rose. 'Why?'

'New task orders came through this morning. We leave for Sumatra in three days' time.'

'Dammit, Rory. I knew this would happen! Why you? Why now? What about the leave they approved two months ago?' Erin paced the length of the car, turned, and paced back. Rory was an Army Engineer and wedded to his work. Questioning his choice of career or the Army's decision-making was pointless. 'Scratch those questions. Does Mum know?'

'We're only rebuilding infrastructure, Erin. It won't be dangerous.'

'So she doesn't know.'

Rory sighed. 'I'll tell her tonight. At dinner. You will come, won't you?'

'No!' She ran a hand through her hair, knowing full

well that her refusal to go to dinner would be short-lived. Rory always took them out to dinner whenever notice to move orders came in. It was a family tradition. Her father, a Rear Admiral, always took them out to dinner whenever *his* deployment orders came in too. Hell, the defence forces probably had a protocol booklet outlining exactly how to deliver such news to loved ones. It probably said, *Make sure you're in a public place and feed them first.* 'Dammit, Rory, it better be somewhere expensive because you owe me big. My collection's due in a month. I need those stones!'

'I'm sorry, Erin. If you can find someone else to go with you, preferably a eunuch with the protective instincts of a Rottweiler, you can still take the car.'

'Gee, who to ask? The list is so long.'

'I see your point,' he said. 'Okay, you can widen the search criteria to include females. But she still has to be capable of covering your back.'

'I could go alone.'

'Only if you intend paying by card and getting the stones shipped to you. That could work.'

'Don't do this to me, Rory.' He knew as well as she did that the best stones were found in the most unlikely places—the one-man mines where you could forget bank cards and delivery options. Out on those claims they traded stones for cash and that was it. 'There's no one in your unit staying behind who you could con into coming with me?'

'Absolutely not!'

Erin sighed. She had an ironclad resistance to military men. Why Rory felt the need to protect her from them was a mystery. 'Maybe I'll put an ad in the paper.'

'Over my dead body,' he said. And then, 'Dinner's at Doyle's. Just so you know.'

Harbourside views and the best seafood selection in Sydney. He did have guilt. 'What time?' she countered. 'Just in case I can make it.'

'Seven-thirty, and if you're not there I'm coming to find you,' he said, and hung up.

Great, just great. Erin scowled as she ended the call and tossed the phone on the front seat. Her passenger had retrieved his bag and was regarding her with a tilt to his lips that told her he'd found the show amusing. Lucky him.

'Problems?' he murmured.

'Yeah, but I'm working on a solution.' She had other options. She could buy stones at auction or off the Internet. But she wouldn't get value for money and her chances of finding something that little bit different would be slim. No. Not good enough. The design competition she'd entered was a prestigious one. Reputations were made there. Careers forged. She needed six perfect pieces of jewellery and for that she needed perfect stones. 'You're not a eunuch, are you?'

'I'm not even going to ask where that question came from,' he said.

'It's just that I need a co-driver,' she said in a rush and his gaze slid to the chauffeurs cap on the front seat. 'Not for the taxi. For a gem-buying trip out west. And not just any driver. He has to be built like, er, well, like you. For bodyguarding and safe gemkeeping purposes. I don't suppose you'd be interested in coming along?'

He looked surprised.

And then he looked stern.

'You should be more careful,' he said. 'What would your brother say if he knew you'd just asked a complete stranger to accompany you on this trip?'

'I really don't want to dwell on it.' Desperation obviously did strange things to a woman. She had no idea who he was or what he did for a living and absolutely no idea what had possessed her to ask him on this trip. So she was impulsive, always had been. She wasn't normally *this* impulsive. 'You're right,' she said. 'Bad idea. Forget I asked.'

'I wouldn't recommend an ad in the paper, either.'

'You're not alone.' Ten to one he had a sister stashed away somewhere. 'Don't let me keep you.'

'How much do I owe you?'

'Nothing. The meter wasn't running.' He had that look about him, a stubborn slant to his chin that told her he was going to be difficult about this. 'Okay then. Answer a question for me and we're square.'

'You want to know what I do?'

'What makes you think that?' He levelled a look at her that made her want to laugh. Damn, but he was appealing when he wasn't being melancholy. 'I'd rather know your name.'

The silence that followed was awkward, to say the least. He didn't want to tell her.

'Never mind,' she said with a rueful shake of her head. She should have known better. Did know better. There was just something about him that made her want to know more. 'Slate's clean. Have a nice day.'

'Tristan,' he said gruffly as she went to get in the car. 'Tristan Bennett.'

There was power in a name so carefully given. Erin halted and stared at him in silence. Those marvellous toffee-coloured eyes of his were guarded and the expression on his face was wry, as if he'd surprised himself with his revelation. Such a small, everyday thing, the giving of a name. Except that now that she'd won it from him she had no idea what to do with it.

'Well, Tristan Bennett,' she said finally. 'Welcome home.'

CHAPTER TWO

TRISTAN didn't want her to go. Maybe it was curiosity or maybe it was just that he was putting off stepping through that front door and into his childhood, but now that she was on the verge of leaving he was looking for ways to keep her there. 'What do you need the gems for?' he asked.

'When I'm not driving taxis I make jewellery,' Erin said. 'There's a competition coming up in four weeks' time, a prestigious one, and for that I need good stones.'

A jeweller? He wouldn't have picked it. 'You're not wearing any jewellery.'

'Company policy. There's less to rob.'

Good policy, he thought. 'So when were you planning on making this trip?'

'Next Monday.'

One week away. 'Well, if you can't find anyone you know to go with you, let me know. Maybe I can help.' What was he saying? Why was he offering to help her? He wasn't *that* good a Samaritan. Obviously he was more jet-lagged than he thought.

She was looking at him with her head cocked to one side. 'You're very sweet, aren't you? Underneath it all.'

Sweet? No one had ever called him sweet before. He tried the word on for size, found it an uncomfortable fit. 'No.'

'Suit yourself,' she said. 'Anyway, better get going. Places to go.'

She was leaving. 'You haven't told me *your* name yet.'

'You don't want to know my name.'

'I don't?'

'No. Not really.' Her smile was rueful. 'But I'll tell you anyway. It's Erin. Erin Sinclair.'

It took Erin five days to admit defeat. Friends, cousins, distant cousins…they were all busy. Maybe if she'd been able to give them more notice she'd have had better luck, but she didn't have that luxury. The competition pieces had to be ready in a month. She was running out of time, almost out of options. Almost.

There was still Tristan Bennett.

He was everything she needed. Tough, protective, and determined to keep his distance. He'd said he might be able to help.

Maybe it was time to find out what he meant.

Erin debated hard over what to wear. She wanted her dealings with Tristan to be businesslike so she decided on beige trousers, flat sandals, and a collared shirt. Never mind that the shirt was a deep, vibrant pink and that the neckline dipped low. To her way of thinking, creamy skin and cleavage was simply a backdrop for more important things.

Like jewellery.

She opted for one of her favourite necklaces: a slim

column of polished jade with a freeform platinum swirl oversetting it. Erin knew the history of jewellery all the way back to Mesopotamia. The materials, the motifs, the meanings and the making of them. Her designs were good. Different. In her more confident moments she even thought she had a shot at winning this competition.

With the right stones, the right design, flawless execution…

One step at a time.

To make a tough job easier you carved it up. You set goals and time frames, and attacked it systematically. Her father had taught her that when he'd tried to instill in her a respect for military ways and military ideals. He thought she hadn't listened, thought he'd failed her when she'd told him she wanted to design jewellery rather than weaponry, but he was wrong. He hadn't failed her and she had listened. First things first. One step at a time.

She needed the right stones. And for that she needed Tristan Bennett.

One-ninety-two Albany Street looked different with the lawn mowed and the garden tamed. He'd let the climbing rose have its way along the verandah, and he'd left the autumn leaves beneath the old oak trees, but it was big-picture tidy and all the more appealing for those things he'd let be.

It wasn't until Erin pulled into the driveway and brought the car to a halt that she saw him. He was on a ladder braced against the side of the house, scooping leaves from the gutter. Man at work. And then his gaze connected with hers as she got out of the car and the leaf scooping stopped.

'Erin Sinclair,' he said as she came to a halt not far from the ladder and Erin smiled up at him. He'd asked her her name out of pure politeness but at least he remembered it.

'You've been cleaning,' she said. 'You do good work.'

'You're back,' he countered. 'I wondered if you would be.'

'You're a hard man to forget.' Easy to dream about though.

'You couldn't find anyone to go with you on your trip out west, could you?'

'No,' she admitted as he came down the ladder, first his boots and then the rest of him. 'But you are hard to forget.' He was bigger than she remembered him, his skin a touch browner. A sun-kissed dark angel, she thought, and wondered if every woman who saw him got that little bit breathless or if it was just her. He slipped his heavy-duty gloves off and slung them over a rung of the ladder, revealing his strong, square hands. Hands that would know their way around a woman's body.

'I still need a co-driver,' she said, trying hard not to think about how those hands would feel rushing all over *her*. 'And I was wondering if you'd be interested in the position. I'll pay for your meals and accommodation, of course, and maybe we can come to some arrangement regarding payment for your time. It wouldn't be much, but if you're currently, er, looking for work, every little bit helps, right?'

'I don't need your money,' he said. 'Save it for your purchases.'

'So you're not out of work?'

'I'm currently on leave from my work.'

Whatever that was. Not exactly forthcoming when it came to talking about himself, she'd noticed that before. 'I'm expecting the trip to take four or five days, depending on what I find and when. The first stop is Lightning Ridge for opals. After that I want to head over to Inverell to look at the sapphires.'

'I can manage a few days.'

'You can? Just like that?'

Her smile was like sunshine, her warmth drawing Tristan in even as he moved away. She was too open, far too trusting. Everything he wasn't.

'There's just one problem,' she said. 'I don't know you all that well. I'll need to run some sort of check on you.'

Maybe not that trusting, he amended, applauding her good sense. 'How?'

'I'm thinking of taking you to dinner.'

Dinner? Tristan stared at her in disbelief. 'You call a *dinner* date a foolproof method of taking a man's measure?'

'You're right,' she said. 'It needs tweaking. We'll have it at my mother's.'

'Your…' What? 'Oh, no. No.' He shook his head for emphasis. 'I don't do dinner with other people's families.'

'It's just my mother,' she said soothingly. 'Possibly my grandmother as well.'

Two mothers. 'Absolutely not!'

'Well, I can't very well go haring off with a complete stranger for a week without someone in my family knowing who I'm with, can I?'

'You should meet my sister,' he said darkly. 'What about

your father? Can't I meet him instead? Or your brother?'
Brothers he could deal with. He had three of them.

'They're out of the country. Besides, they can be a
little overprotective about these things. Mothers are far
more reasonable. Say seven o'clock tonight?'

'No.'

'When, then?'

Never. 'What if I gave you my driver's licence?' he
said. 'You can discover a lot about a person from their
driver's licence.'

'Like what? That they can drive?'

'Their full name and address. Their date of birth.
With that you can access other records.'

'You're not a criminal, are you?'

'Not yet.'

She looked at him through eyes that were clear and
thoughtful and not nearly as guileless as she would have
him believe. 'Okay, I'll cut you a deal. Sunday brunch but
it's still at my mother's. In the interests of fairness you can
bring your mother too.'

Tristan shook his head. 'My mother died a long time
ago.' He'd been twelve.

Startled silence greeted his statement and Tristan
waited warily for her reaction. This wasn't information
he usually offered up. He hated the sympathy that came
with it; that soft, nurturing look women got in their eyes
when they found out. He was thirty years old. He did
not need mothering.

'Guess that's out of the question, then,' she said at
last. 'What about your sister?'

'She lives in England.'

Erin Sinclair sighed and the pretty little pendant dangling from the chain around her neck seemed to sigh right along with her. 'I don't suppose you have a spinster aunt nearby who loves nothing more than to talk about your childhood escapades?'

'No, but the next-door neighbour's cockatoo remembers me. I could bring him.'

'Now we're getting somewhere,' she said. 'Bring the neighbours as well.'

Relentless wasn't usually a word he applied to whimsical women with laughter in their eyes, but in this case it seemed to fit. 'Couldn't you just trust your own judgement?'

'I am. It says never trust a man who refuses to meet your mother.'

She had a point.

'Last chance,' she said. 'Brunch tomorrow morning. You can even set a time limit. Say, half an hour?'

Still he hesitated.

'If I have to find someone else to come with me on this trip, I will.'

'You're bluffing.'

Her hands went to her hips; her gaze was steady. She bluffed very well. He found, disturbingly, that he kind of liked the idea of a week out west, hunting down gemstones with Erin Sinclair. 'How many mothers?' he said at last.

'Just the one if it makes you any feel better.'

It did. Surely he could manage one mother for half an hour. It wasn't as if they were dating. No. All he had to do was meet the woman, reassure her that he'd look out for her daughter, thank her for the coffee, and leave. 'One mother, half an hour,' he said firmly. 'Maximum.'

'No problem.' Her smile was warm. 'I'll pick you up at ten o clock?'

'Give me the address and I'll meet you there.' His father's car was in the garage. It could use the run. Although... He turned his attention to the five-point-seven-litre, eight-cylinder, factory-modified Monaro sitting in his driveway. Now *that* was a very sweet ride. 'Yours?'

'Rory's,' she said and started towards it. Tristan followed willingly. 'I don't have a car. He offered to let me take it on the trip but I figured if I did, the sellers would take one look at it and triple the price of the stones. I've decided to take my mother's Ford instead. She can drive the Monaro.'

'I think I'm going to weep.'

'You would if you had to put fuel in it.'

'You see, that's where you're wrong. We're talking sledgehammer acceleration and a top speed guaranteed to make your eyes water. The price of fuel is secondary.'

'You sound just like my brother,' she said as she fished a cardboard drink coaster and a pen from the Monaro, set the coaster face down on the roof of the car, and started writing on it. 'What is it with men and fast cars?'

Tristan winced. 'Mind the duco.'

'I swear, it's like an echo,' she muttered, her attention still on her task. 'Why do you think I'm using a coaster?'

'This is a good idea, right?' asked Erin the following morning as she set a packet of freshly ground coffee and a bar cake down on her mother's kitchen bench. She hadn't lived at home for over two years but she'd never quite kicked the habit of visiting her mother's kitchen on a regular basis. It was the perfect place to sit and chill and, when necessary, grill potential travelling companions. 'It seemed like a good idea at the time.'

'Very sensible, dear.' Lillian Sinclair regarded her daughter over the top of a pair of purple-framed reading glasses. The glasses bordered on the theatrical; the eyes behind them were shrewd. 'What was his name again?'

'Tristan Bennett.'

'I knew a Tristan once. He was a dance choreographer. Darling man.'

'I don't think this one's a dance choreographer.' Not that she knew for sure, but the thought of Tristan Bennett mincing the floorboards in tight tights and a V-necked T-shirt didn't really work for her. 'Tristan's a misleading name for this particular man.'

'Oh? What name would you have given him?'

'I'm thinking Lucifer.'

Her mother's eyebrows rose. 'That's quite a name.'

'He's very handsome.' She thought her mother needed at least some advance warning.

'What about wicked?'

'I hope not.' Erin hesitated. 'Instinct tells me he's a good man. It also tells me he's no stranger to the dark side.'

'A man doesn't have to be part of the darkness to walk through it.' Big fan of Chinese poetry, her mother. 'What does he do for a living?'

'No idea.'

'You should have asked.'

'I intend to ask.' Erin slit the packet of coffee open with a knife. No more waltzing around the subject. She needed to know. 'He's just so… elusive.'

The doorbell rang. It was ten o clock. 'Punctual, though,' said her mother. 'I like that in a man.'

'How do I look?'

'Fresh. How do you want to look?'

She was wearing casual green trousers and a sleeveless cotton top in pale pink. A dozen thin Indian-style gold bangles danced along one wrist. 'I was aiming for businesslike with a twist.'

'I think you overdid the twist,' said her mother. 'Do you want me to answer the door or will you?'

'I'll get it,' she said with a sigh, and headed up the hallway.

He was wearing a white business shirt. The top two buttons were undone and the sleeves were rolled to his elbows, but it *was* a business shirt. The rest of his clothes were what she'd come to expect: comfortable-looking cargo trousers, well-worn boots…

There was sulphur-crested cockatoo sitting in a cage at his feet.

'This is Pat,' he said. 'Unfortunately the neighbours had to go to church.'

O-kay. 'Come on through.'

He picked up the birdcage, followed her through to the kitchen, and Erin watched with fatalistic resignation as her mother took one look at Tristan and Pat and fell in love with them both. When the introductions had been made, when Tristan was sitting at the breakfast counter with Pat sitting next to him, and Erin was brewing up the coffee, Lillian Sinclair sat opposite Tristan and favoured him with a long, assessing look from over the top of her glasses.

'Cake?' she offered.

'Thank you.'

She cut him a thick slice. Pat got wholegrain bread with a slather of honey.

'No swearing,' said the parrot by way of thank you.

'Not in my kitchen,' said Lillian affably. 'So, Tristan, Erin tells me you've been living in London.'

'Yes.'

He looked uncomfortable, Erin decided. He hadn't touched his cake. She brought the coffee pot over to the counter, found mugs for everyone. 'Black, two sugars, right?' she said as she poured the coffee.

'Right.'

'Eat,' said Lillian, gesturing towards the cake. 'You look like you could use some nourishment.'

With an oddly defenceless glance in her mother's direction, Tristan picked up his piece of cake and ate. 'It's good,' he said after a man-sized mouthful.

'It should be,' said Erin. 'I bought it from the corner deli.' There were shadows in his eyes this morning. Shadows under them. 'You look like you could use some sleep as well.'

'I sleep fine.' He finished his cake, reached for his coffee. 'I eat plenty.'

'Hell,' said Pat. 'Purgatory.'

'He's Catholic,' said Tristan.

'He's forgiven,' said her mother. 'What brings you back to Australia?'

Tristan shrugged. 'Whim. I had some leave owing. I decided to come home.'

There was more to it than that, thought Erin. Maybe he'd been worked over by a woman. 'How long will you be staying?' she asked him.

'Six weeks.'

Six weeks was a lot of time to be away from a job. Any job. She knew it was rude to ask a person what they did for a living, but she had the feeling that if she didn't ask him outright he'd evade the subject for ever. 'What exactly is it that you do?'

'I work for Interpol.'

Erin stared at him, open-mouthed. *Not* what she'd been expecting. 'Paper pusher?' she asked finally.

'No.'

No.

'Damnation,' said the parrot.

'Now, now, Pat. It's not that bad,' Lillian told the bird. 'He could have been Navy.' That would have really annoyed her.

'An Interpol cop,' said Erin flatly. 'You.'

'Why? Is that a problem?'

'Only for your future *wife*.' He was watching her intently. Her mother was eyeing her with something very close to sympathy. Tristan Bennett was a cop. Serve and protect and all that went with it. Another man with secrets to keep and a job that came before family. Why on earth hadn't she seen it sooner? All the signs had been there. The strength, the aloofness, the quiet authority...

'At least you'll be safe on your trip,' said her mother.

'Yeah.' *Damn* him. Why couldn't he have been a stockbroker or a tax accountant? 'Why police work?'

'I like justice,' he said quietly. 'I enjoy the chase.'

'Do you always get your man?'

'No. Not always.' He looked away but not before Erin had seen the frustration in his eyes, along with an underlying anguish that clear took her breath away. Ditch the failed-relationship theory. Tristan Bennett had been worked over by his work.

Great, just great. Now she wanted to *comfort* him. So did her mother. Her mother cut him another piece of cake. Her mother had been married to a military man for twenty-eight years; her firstborn had followed in his father's footsteps. Taciturn, soul-wounded warriors were Lillian Sinclair's speciality.

'Here's where I need to get to,' said Erin, fishing a map from a pile of papers and spreading it out on the counter. She knew a thing or two about distracting wounded warriors herself. 'I was thinking we could take the inland road.'

'You'll be driving straight past the Warrambungles, then,' said her mother. 'You could go climbing.' She eyed Tristan speculatively. 'You're about Rory's size, give or take a couple of kilos. You can use his gear.'

'You climb?' asked Tristan, looking from her mother to her.

'Sinclair family sport. I've been climbing since I could crawl.' It wouldn't hurt to pack the gear in the back, just in case. 'Do you climb?'

'No.'

'Would you like to? We can go as easy or as hard as

you like. Your call. I figure you for the vertical limit, do-it-or-die-trying type, but I could be wrong.'

'Wonderful sport, climbing,' said Lillian. 'Challenges the body, clears the mind, and then there's all that spectacular scenery thrown in for free. I don't know why it isn't more popular. More cake?'

'Who *are* you people?' said Tristan.

'Hey,' said Erin indignantly. 'You're the one who brought the parrot.'

Half an hour with Erin and her mother passed quickly. Lillian Sinclair had a knack for making even the wariest of people relax, decided Tristan, even if she had been persistent about feeding him. Sandwiches had followed the cake. Thick crusty Vienna loaf sandwiches with rare roast beef, salad greens, homegrown tomatoes, and mustard. She'd made him two of those and he'd made short work of them. He'd been hungry. Hungrier than he thought.

Oh, they'd grilled him. Lillian Sinclair knew of his father through some art gallery who'd consulted him on Chinese pottery pieces so they talked about him for a while. He'd told them of his three brothers, all of them older, and his younger sister. They'd talked about London and Kensington Gardens, the River Thames and the gentrification of Chelsea, where he had his apartment. Rock climbing, yoga, children's book illustrations, and the merits of super-sharp kitchen knives. All had been touched on and considered.

Not your average family.

'See?' said Erin as she walked him and Pat out to the car. 'That wasn't so bad, was it?'

'It was bearable.'

'Nah, you liked sitting in my mother's kitchen. Everyone does. You just won't admit it.'

She was right. But he still wasn't going to admit it. 'So you've taken my measure. What now?'

'Pack for a week and I'll pick you up in the morning,' she said as he bundled Pat into the passenger seat. 'Unless you've changed your mind.'

'I haven't,' he said, but he thought she might have. 'Have you?'

'No.'

She looked pensive. He thought he knew why. 'You don't much like what I do for a living, do you?'

'I'm sure you're very good at what you do,' she said coolly.

She smelled of sunshine and lemons, and her slim little body seemed tiny when compared to his, but he had her measure now, just as she had his. She was pure steel. 'You haven't answered my question.'

Her eyes grew stormy. 'Arrest me.'

She had a smart mouth. Lush, unpainted, sexy. He liked looking at it. He was looking at it now. 'What is it that you don't like?'

'It doesn't matter,' she said with a toss of her head. 'I only want you for your gem-guarding skills. I've decided against wanting you for anything else.'

'Really?'

'Yes. You're an intriguing man, don't get me wrong. But you're not my type.'

'Are you quite finished?' he asked silkily.

'I think so.' She tucked a stray strand of shiny brown hair behind her ear and nodded. 'Yep. All done.'

'Good, because I have this theory.'

'Scientists have theories.'

'Cops have them too. You see, I think you're attracted to me. Lord knows, for some strange reason I'm attracted to you. Want to test my theory?'

'No.'

But her cheeks were flushed, and when he traced her lips with his fingers they parted for him. Soft, so soft, he'd known they would be. The pulse at the base of her neck was beating frantically, he found the spot with his fingers and watched with no little satisfaction as her lashes fluttered closed and her breathing grew ragged.

'I don't want you,' she said.

'I can see that.' He gave her every opportunity to move away as he slid his hand around the back of her neck and closed the gap between their lips. She didn't move towards him, not one little bit, but she shuddered when his lips touched hers and that was all the encouragement he needed. Once. Twice. And then again.

It was the third time that did it.

He thought he was in control. Just a quick taste of her, that was all he'd take. Just to prove that she was no different from any other woman, certainly no sweeter. That it was all in his imagination. He was still in control when she slid her hands to his shoulders. Still coherent when he pulled her towards him. And then their bodies touched and fire streaked through him as her lips opened beneath his and then he knew.

She wasn't sweet.

She wasn't like any other woman he'd ever known. And his control deserted him.

Deeper, she took him there and he thought he might drown in her desire. More, she gave it to him and he shuddered at the extent of her generosity. She reached up and sank her fingers into his hair and offered him more again. Nothing mattered but the woman in his arms and the magic they created. Nothing.

He'd been kissing women for half a lifetime, but not like this. Never like this.

Abruptly he released her.

Her lips were swollen, her eyes bewildered, as they stared at one another in shocked silence.

'*Hell*,' he muttered, taking a giant step back and shoving his hands in his pocket to stop himself reaching for her again. 'You're not my type either.'

Erin made it back to her mother's kitchen without her legs giving way. That was the good news. The bad news was that her mother took one look at her and just plain *knew* what she and Tristan Bennett had been up to. 'I think I just had an epiphany,' she said as she slumped down onto the stool Tristan had vacated. 'Seriously. The earth moved, fireworks lit up the sky, and I'm pretty sure I heard harps playing in the heavens.'

'That's interesting,' said her mother. 'Tristan hear them too?'

'I don't know. He left in a hurry.' Nought to sixty in three seconds flat. In a Corolla.

'I liked him,' said her mother.

'He's all wrong,' countered Erin. 'I should ring him and cancel the trip. I'll just have to buy stones at auction, that's all. There's one on Friday.'

'Good idea,' said Lillian. 'You might even find stones you like that you can afford this time round. Not that you ever have before.'

Erin sighed heavily. 'He's a cop.'

'An elite cop. A Criminal Investigation Officer, I think you'll find.'

'Go on. Rub it in.'

'The trouble with you is you can't see past his occupation.'

The trouble *was* she'd been intrigued by him from the start and his occupation didn't seem to matter a damn. Now she was even more fascinated by him, and that was a bad idea for a girl who wanted a husband who came home every night and wasn't compelled to keep secrets from his family. 'Is it so bad to want to fall in love with a man whose work *doesn't* take him all over the globe hunting down bad guys?'

'Not at all,' murmured Lillian. They'd had this conversation before. 'I'm the first to admit it can wear thin at times. But a passionate crusader won't be satisfied with menial work, Erin. The two just don't go together.'

'I don't want a passionate crusader.'

'Sweetie, you imprinted on them at birth. I doubt you'll settle for anything else.'

'I'll marry a doctor, then. At least they get to stay at home while they save the world.'

'Yeah. Those doctors have it so easy. Eighteen-hour days, life or death decisions to make, needy patients…

Their wives have it easy too. Special occasions are never interrupted by a call from the hospital and their husbands are always home at six every night, bright, cheerful, and ready to help cook dinner.'

'Okay, so maybe that wasn't such a good example.'

'Life's a balancing act, Erin. You have work that you're passionate about too. Find the right man and the balance will come, no matter what he does for a living. As for Tristan Bennett, he's available, suitable, and willing to help you achieve your goals. He's exactly what you need. Make sure he eats.'

Oh, please! 'He's a grown man. He'll eat when he's hungry.' Erin frowned and drummed her fingers on the counter. There was something else bothering her about Tristan Bennett apart from his incredible kisses—something big. 'He's running from something,' she said finally. 'A botched case. A bad call. He's hurting.'

'I noticed that.' Her mother eyed her steadily. 'He responds to you.'

'Reluctantly.'

'But he does respond.'

CHAPTER THREE

HALF an hour. That was all it had taken Erin and Lillian Sinclair to unravel him, thought Tristan darkly as he wove his way home through the leafy suburban streets. Hell, the last time he'd been played so skilfully was in his Interpol recruitment interview six years ago; back when he'd been naive, idealistic and a whole lot more malleable than he was now. He liked to think he'd matured a little since then. He liked to think he'd grown smarter. Not that the last half-hour was any indication. Anyone witnessing that little debacle could be forgiven for thinking he wasn't smart at all.

He thought back, tried to pinpoint how they'd slipped through his guard, but he came up empty. He'd sat down on that stool, Lillian had looked at him, Erin had dumped two loaded spoonfuls of sugar into his coffee cup, and he'd been history. 'See what stress does to you?' he told the cockatoo. 'You don't eat, you don't sleep, and you say yes to things you'd never usually agree to.' Like brunch and week-long gem-buying trips. 'Then you go and kiss a woman who doesn't like cops, mainly to annoy her, and end up misplacing your mind.'

Tristan slowed for a roundabout. 'Stay away from women, Pat. That's my advice to you.'

Pat ignored him completely. Pat was busy preening feathers. It occurred to him, belatedly, that Pat might just be a *female* cockatoo—which meant that from the tender age of nine he'd been spilling all his innermost secrets and no few kissing fantasies to a *girl*. '*Patricia?*'

Pat stopped preening feathers to look at him with a beady eye. 'Hallelujah, brother.'

Whoa! Definitely a female. How could he have *missed* it? All of a sudden, Tristan's world had tilted off course and it didn't seem to matter which way he looked, nothing was what it seemed.

He'd been looking forward to this road trip. Opals, sapphires, miles of road, and the company of a beautiful woman with a smart mouth and an easy smile…He'd wanted the distraction, wondered where it might lead, and he'd fanned the spark between him and the pixie deliberately. Hell, he was only human.

But he'd been thinking light-hearted. A pleasant diversion, for heaven's sake, not full on enslavement.

She didn't like what he did for a living.

Snap. Right now, neither did he.

He lived in London.

In a two-bedroom flat with the city all around him and no room to breathe. If he quit his job there was nothing keeping him in London. He could go anywhere, do anything. He could come home.

He was scared witless of giving his heart to a woman and then losing her.

There was that.

Sometimes a man's fear was buried so deep that it couldn't be reached and it couldn't be conquered. It just was. It certainly didn't need a reason for being, although Tristan figured his was tied up with losing his mother and watching his father crumble. Oh, his father had rallied, they all had, but there was no denying that the loss of his mother was engraved on his heart. Then he'd watched Jake marry young, watched his brother struggle to keep his dream alive and Jianna happy, only to have her leave him six months later. Sweet, loving Jianna, who'd been a part of their lives since before he could remember, had turned tail and fled, taking the best part of Jake with her.

Tristan liked women. Warm, smart women who could make a man laugh. Sharp, serious women who knew what they wanted to do with their lives and weren't afraid to work towards it. He liked them all, liked being with them, enjoyed making love to them. As long as they didn't get too close.

With Erin it was different. He looked at Erin and something stirred inside him. Something potent and unfamiliar and powerful enough to declare war on his old and constant companion that was fear.

Not love. Not yet.

Desire, maybe. The kind that went soul deep and left a man aching and needy. Not love, never that. His brain shied away from the notion, determined to resist it.

While his heart trembled.

Erin couldn't sleep. The memory of Tristan's kisses and her newfound knowledge of his occupation kept her tossing and turning long after she should have been asleep. He was all wrong, no matter what her mother thought. Her mother was wrong. He was too intense, too intriguing, too much *everything* for her peace of mind.

He kissed like an angel.

Erin glanced at the clock. Not quite midnight. She should call him. Tell him she'd changed her mind about needing his company on this trip. She was a grown woman. A smart woman. Far better to make this trip alone and take her chances than lose her heart to the likes of Tristan Bennett.

No. He'd looked tired. It was far too late to call him now. What if he were asleep? What if this was his first decent sleep in weeks and she woke him? Besides, she didn't have his number. Maybe *she* should go to sleep. There was plenty of time to call him in the morning. Erin turned over, rearranged her pillow, and closed her eyes.

Nope. Not working.

Two minutes later she had Tristan's number, or more accurately his father's number, and was standing by her bed, cordless phone in hand, listening for a dial tone. She punched the numbers in quickly, before she changed her mind, and waited for him to pick up. She could do this. All she had to do was calmly tell him the trip was off, everything would go back to normal, and then she could get some sleep.

Five rings. Six rings.

And then the ringing stopped.

'Bennett.' Tristan's voice was a sleepy rasp. The downside was that she'd woken him. The upside was that he'd get to sleep late tomorrow morning. She was pretty sure he'd appreciate the trade off. Eventually.

'It's Erin,' she said, starting to pace the room. 'I'm having second thoughts about this trip.'

'Fine,' he muttered. 'Goodnight.'

'Wait!' So much for calm. 'Aren't you going to ask me *why* I'm having second thoughts?'

'No.'

'I mean, you can't just kiss a girl like that and expect her to carry on as though it never happened. I think I deserve an explanation.'

'There is no explanation,' he said. 'It's one of life's little jokes.'

'Not laughing.'

'Trust me, it won't happen again.'

'Damn right it won't!'

'Pixies don't swear,' he said.

'I'm not a pixie. About this trip—'

'Does that mean we're done with the kissing talk?'

'Unless you'd like to tell me that our kiss was absolutely perfect and that you can hardly eat, breathe, or sleep for thinking about it, yes.'

'Moving on,' he said.

Right. Where was she? Oh, yeah. What to do about the trip. She stopped pacing in favour of sitting cross-legged in the middle of the bed. 'I'm thinking of cancelling this trip.'

'Because of the kissing?'

'Not at all. We're done talking about the kissing, remember?'

'Sorry. My mistake.' He sounded slightly more awake, a whole lot more amused. 'Why are you cancelling?'

Because of the kissing. Because of the potential for

more kissing. 'I heard there were some good stones coming up for auction this week. I figure I'll get those instead.'

'Liar,' he said. 'But it was a good try.'

'How do you know I'm lying?'

'I'm a cop.'

She hadn't forgotten. 'What kind of cop?' She didn't expect a straight answer. She just wanted to see what he'd say. 'What exactly is it that you do?'

'I investigate international car theft.' He was all the way awake now; she could hear it in his voice.

'Do you ever work undercover?'

'Sometimes.'

'Ever talk about it?'

'No.'

Surprise, surprise. Maybe she *could* manage a week in his company. Clearly, he had no intention of following through on that kiss. And if *he* kept his distance, then surely she could. Maybe she'd been a bit hasty about cancelling the trip; maybe she *wouldn't* lose her heart to him after all. 'It probably wouldn't hurt to take a look at those opals out at Lightning Ridge, anyway. Just in case.'

Tristan sighed heavily. 'Why don't you sleep on it and call me in the morning?'

'Well, I'd like to. Really. It's just that I'm having a little trouble sleeping. I'd rather sort it out now and then sleep.'

'Wouldn't we all?' he said darkly.

Not a man bent on seduction. That was good. And she hadn't once pictured him lying there in a big old bed, on a mass of white cotton sheets, surrounded by fluffy white pillows that were a perfect foil for his eyes, that face, and that gloriously hard body of his.

'Erin?'

His voice was soft, sexy. Pity about the underlying thread of impatience. 'What?'

'Make up your mind.'

Cue the unmistakable air of command. Not that she was impressed by that. She was immune to weary warriors who wore command as if they were born to it and reticence like a shield. 'We're going.' There, she'd done it. She'd made her decision.

'Are you sure?'

'I'll pick you up at eight o'clock. Just like we planned. This morning's kiss was an aberration. I see that now.'

'That's a relief,' he said, and hung up.

Erin was awake before dawn the next morning. Now that she had her feelings for Tristan sorted out—breathtaking, but not the one for her—she was eager to be underway. She had their lunch prepared and the car packed in record time and only iron control stopped her from hightailing it over to Tristan's two hours earlier than planned.

There was something magical about the start of a trip. Something marvellous about possibilities just waiting to be discovered. The perfect stone and the design she might dream up for it... A long straight stretch of road and a beckoning horizon... People to meet, places to go... Erin glanced at her watch for the umpteenth time in the last fifteen minutes. Five forty-six a.m. She wondered if Tristan was awake yet. Wondered if she should call him and find out.

Probably not. One embarrassing phone call a day was plenty.

It was just on seven-thirty when she reached his house. She was half an hour early but it couldn't be helped. Surely he'd be awake by *now*. She saw an old brass doorbell by the front door, rang it energetically, and stepped back to wait. Twenty seconds, thirty seconds, and then she heard the sound of footsteps coming to the door and then it opened and Tristan stood there wearing nothing but jeans, with his hair wet and tousled and a towel in his hand. Freshly showered and shaved was a *very* good look for him. 'Good. You're nearly ready,' she said, trying hard to ignore his superbly sculpted chest, complete with a sprinkling of dark hair that tapered to a vee. 'Not that I want to rush you.'

'You're early.'

'Only a little.'

Tristan stood aside, silently inviting her to come in. He looked past her, towards her mother's late model Ford, and sighed.

'It's a comfortable ride,' she said reassuringly.

'I know,' he said. 'But it's not quite the Monaro, now, is it?'

'It'll still get us from A to B,' she said firmly. 'Do you have any idea how much attention the Monaro draws on the road? What with the rumble, and the racing wheels... I swear it's a guaranteed trouble magnet.'

'I know.' His grin was swift and decidedly dangerous. 'Why do you think we like it so much?' he said as he shut the door behind her and padded back down the hallway, leaving her to follow in his wake.

Watching Tristan's back muscles flex and ripple as he towel dried his hair on the way down the hall made Erin's hands itch and her mind fog, so she dragged her gaze away from the half-naked Tristan and turned her attention to her surroundings instead, hoping for a distraction. The house was masculine; there was no other word for it. Dark-wood floorboards, a navy hall runner, wood panelling halfway up the walls...The painted part of the walls was a cool forest green. She followed Tristan into what she figured was the living room, only to discover more dark furnishings and walls lined with books. Tristan had mentioned that all his siblings had left home and that his father lived here alone now, but the house still bore the marks of a loved and lived-in family home. She spotted a karate belt behind glass in a cabinet. Now there was a distraction. 'Who's the seventh Dan black belt?'

'Jake. He runs a Martial Arts dojo in Singapore.'

'And the aircraft books?'

'They're Pete's. He's flying charter planes around the Greek islands at the moment. Summer job. It's only temporary.' Tristan didn't seem to mind offering up information about his family, she noted. Just not about himself. There was a photo on the sideboard of a young man in Navy whites who looked disturbingly like Tristan. 'That's Luke,' he said, before she could ask. 'You'd like him. He's a Navy diver.'

Erin bared her teeth. 'So much testosterone,' she said sweetly. 'Anyone in your family have a normal job?'

'Hallie buys and sells ancient Chinese artwork,' he said. 'That's normal.'

Yeah, right. At least he'd stopped towelling his hair. Only now it spiked in places and lay flat in others, framing his face in a way that was boyishly endearing and affording him an innocence that was deceptive. *Very* deceptive. There was nothing innocent about Tristan Bennett. Nothing at all innocent about her body's reaction to his near nakedness and, judging from the way his eyes had darkened and his sudden predatory stillness, he knew exactly what sort of effect he was having on her.

Oh, boy. Not good. Must remember to breathe, she thought, and hurriedly turned her attention to an old framed *The King And I* poster hanging on the wall above the mantelpiece. It was the only vaguely feminine thing in the room. Deborah Kerr teaching Yul Brynner how to waltz. 'I'm assuming the poster belongs to your sister?'

'It's here under sufferance,' said Tristan, seemingly willing to be distracted. 'It used to be Hallie's favourite movie.'

The governess who tamed a proud and strong king. A motherless young girl growing up in a houseful of alpha males. No wonder *The King and I* had been his sister's favourite movie. She'd needed a role model. 'My mother and I caught a rerun at the cinema a few years back,' she said with a wistful sigh. 'It was lovely. I've been a sucker for bald-headed men ever since.'

'Gimme a break,' he said.

Erin eyed his tousled hair critically. Maybe if he didn't have quite so much of it, she wouldn't have this overwhelming urge to bury her hands in it. 'You know, you could use a haircut.'

'I am *not* shaving my head for you.'

'Of course not,' she said soothingly. 'Although—'

'No.'

Right. In that case the bare skin definitely had to go,

because if he didn't cover up soon she was going to start drooling. 'Shouldn't you be getting ready?' she prompted. 'Putting a shirt on?'

'I would if you'd stop asking questions.' His voice was long-suffering.

Erin smiled sweetly. 'I'll wait here. Don't mind me.'

Tristan sent her a warning glance that she decided to ignore and headed for the door. He'd almost reached it when she spoke again. 'So who collects the little toy cars?'

'Models,' he said firmly as he disappeared out the door, taking his tousled hair and his near-naked body with him. 'They're scale replicas.'

'Got it,' she said, not bothering to hide her grin.

The little toy cars were his.

It was like driving with an optimistic fairy, thought Tristan some three hours later. He'd tried silence. He'd tried quelling glances. He'd taken over driving duty. None of it had the slightest impact on Erin's general effervescence. They were aiming for Lightning Ridge that evening, a nine-hundred kilometre trip from Sydney. They weren't even halfway there.

'We could play I Spy,' she said.

'No.'

'Break for lunch?'

'It's not even midday.'

Erin sighed. 'Want to change drivers again?'

He'd been driving for less than an hour. It was nowhere near time to change drivers again. 'No. Put a CD on.' They were between towns. They'd lost radio reception twenty kilometres ago.

'I'm not in the mood for music right now.'

'Perhaps a nap?' he suggested hopefully.

'Maybe after lunch.'

He slid her a sideways glance to see if she was playing him. She was.

'Tell me about yourself,' she said.

'What happened to "Let's not get to know one another"?' he said dryly. They'd decided on that particular tactic about half an hour into the journey. He'd needed something to counteract her effect on him. That ready smile, those laughing eyes. Something, anything, to keep her out.

She was wearing a bright blue T-shirt and casual grey trousers, and there was nothing overtly sexual about them, nothing innately feminine, except that every movement she made *was* feminine, and graceful, and sexy. And then there was the dainty charm bracelet on her arm that accentuated the slenderness of her wrist, the earrings dangling from her ears that drew attention to the delicate curve of her neck, and the pulse he knew he'd find beating there if he put his lips to it.

How on earth was he supposed to get through a week or so of *this*?

'I'm having difficulty with the let's-not-get-to-know-each-other plan,' she said with a sigh. 'I figure if I get to know you I won't find you anywhere near as intriguing. I figure if I'm *really* lucky, I might not even like you.'

There was merit in the idea, he decided warily. Maybe he could even help her out a little. 'What would you like to know?'

'Tell me how you ended up working for Interpol.'

'They had an opening in their stolen car division. They were looking for someone who knew cars. Someone they could send undercover. I qualified.'

'And was it what you expected?'

'It was the wildest game in town. For a while.' He'd thrived on the excitement and the danger, the adrenaline rush that came with each and every takedown.

'So what changed?' she said, her eyes shrewd and far more knowing than he would have liked.

'The odds grew longer, the stakes grew higher, and it stopped becoming a game,' he said quietly. 'I grew up. End of story.'

'That's a terrible story,' she said. 'Don't you have any uplifting stories?'

'Yeah. There was this stolen car ring operating out of Serbia once. Family run business. We knew all the players. We just couldn't touch them. The old man died of a heart attack, the brothers took each other out in the ensuing fight for control, and everyone else lived happily ever after.'

'Gee, thanks for that,' she said with a grimace. 'The kids are going to just love *your* bedtime stories.'

'What kids?'

'Your kids. You are planning on having children, aren't you?'

'I hadn't really thought about it.'

'Not ever?'

'Not yet.'

'You are such a bad bet for a husband.'

'I know,' he said solemnly, stifling a grin. She looked so disgruntled. 'My strengths lie elsewhere.'

'I can't imagine where.'

'Yes, you can.'

She blushed furiously, opened her mouth to speak, caught his eye, and looked away.

Silence. Finally. Tristan grinned, savouring the moment. He loved it when a plan came together.

They stopped for lunch at Gulgong, changed drivers again at Gilgandra, and rolled into Lightning Ridge just as the sun was disappearing behind a desert horizon of red dirt and saltbush. The road sign on the way into the town said, 'Lightning Ridge, Population—?' because, bottom line, no one knew. Rumour had it somewhere between two and twenty thousand. More or less. Lightning Ridge—in the middle of nowhere and chock-full of eccentrics, opal miners, optimists, and fortune seekers—was the perfect place to hide.

'Where are we staying?' he asked.

'We're very flexible in that regard,' she said, shooting him a smile. 'Now would be a good time to decide.'

'I see,' he said, and wondered why the notion that Erin was perfectly comfortable embarking on a journey with no fixed destination in mind disturbed him so much. He *always* travelled this way. His undercover work demanded the flexibility and he just plain preferred it. Women, at least in his experience, did not prefer it. Women always wanted to know where they were headed and when they were going to get there—be it a conversation about a weekend away, or the terms of a relationship. That was just the way it was. 'Let's try this one,' he said, motioning to a motel coming up on their right.

'Done.'

The motel offered air-conditioning, satellite TV, and standby rates. The woman behind the reception desk was frighteningly forthright. 'I can give you a family suite with two rooms and a kitchenette,' she said when Erin asked after accommodation.

'Not two separate rooms?' he asked.

'Take it or leave it.'

'We'll look at it,' he said, and the woman took a key from the hook rack behind her and thumped it down on the desk.

'Last door to the left.'

Erin liked the family suite. It was clean, functional, comfortable, and right there waiting for them at the end of a long day's driving. The bedrooms and bathroom were upstairs, the kitchenette and living area downstairs. If it had been Rory with her on this trip she wouldn't have hesitated, she'd have agreed to stay there without another thought, but it wasn't Rory, this was Tristan and there was a privacy issue to think about. 'What do you think?' she asked tentatively.

Tristan's expression was guarded. 'It's fine.'

They'd just managed nine hours in a car together without finding a whole lot in common apart from an annoyingly persistent physical awareness of one another. Chances were that if he left the lid off the tooth-paste and his towel on the bathroom floor, even that would fade. 'Because we can try somewhere else if you'd rather.'

'This is fine.' In that remote way of his that promised distance no matter how aware they might be of one another.

'We'll take it,' Erin told the woman back at reception.

'What name?'

'Sinclair,' she said.

Tristan said, 'Smith.'

'Sinclair Smith,' said the woman dryly. 'Is that hyphenated?'

'Yes,' said Tristan.

'I'll need a car registration number as well,' she said, and Tristan rattled it off.

'Handy,' said Erin.

'Occupational hazard.'

'Who's paying?' asked the woman.

'I am,' said Erin, fishing her credit card from her wallet. Tristan frowned and looked as if he was going to protest and Erin shot him a warning glance. She was paying for the accommodation. They'd discussed it already. 'Two nights should do it.'

'Stay three and I'll throw in a free double pass to the town pool as well.'

Gee, the town pool. Huge incentive.

'Maybe three nights,' said Tristan with a lopsided smile that had the formerly forthright receptionist smiling coquettishly and patting her beehive hairdo into place, never mind that she was old enough to be his grandmother. 'We'll let you know.'

It didn't take long to unload. Tristan had his carryall. Erin had a backpack full of clothes, a cotton shoulder bag with her jeweller's loupe and a sketchpad and pencils, and a box of assorted groceries to bring in. Two trips, except that Tristan hauled her backpack out of the car along with his carryall, which left her with just the groceries and the shoulder bag. Rory would have done the same and Erin would have accepted his assistance automatically and thought nothing of it. That was what brothers did.

When Tristan did it she grew decidedly weak at the knees.

'Do you want the room with the double bed in it or the one with the two singles?' he asked from upstairs as she unloaded the grocery box in the kitchenette.

'What colour are the sheets on the double bed?'

'White.'

Damn.

'They're all white,' he said, appearing in the kitchenette doorway. 'Is that a problem?'

'Not really.' Who was she kidding? It didn't matter what colour the bedsheets were, Tristan Bennett would look sensational on them. Of course, he'd look a lot less sensational wedged into a single bed but she didn't really have the heart to make him sleep in one. He was bigger than she was. Gloriously, mesmerisingly bigger. She took a deep breath, blew it out again, and pushed all thoughts of white sheets, big beds, and Tristan Bennet aside. 'I'll take the single.' There. Bedrooms sorted. Bedroom doors firmly closed. 'What shall we do about dinner? Eat in or go out?'

'What's in the box?' he asked.

'Breakfast food, mainly. A few snacks. A couple of bottles of wine. Nothing that could constitute dinner. It's more a question of bringing take-away back here or finding somewhere to sit down and eat. Depends what you feel like eating. And before we go any further, I'm paying for it.'

'You don't need to do that.'

He wasn't comfortable with a woman picking up the tab for him. The deeply hidden, feminine part of her soul, which saw a man as both provider and protector, applauded him. But she wasn't about to let him pay for his own meals. Not without an argument, at any rate. 'Think of yourself as a business expense,' she said. 'Me, I'm thinking hamburgers. How about you?'

'A works hamburger, heavy on the BBQ sauce,' he said. 'And your accountant is *never* going to see me as a business expense. Just so you know.' He fished a fifty-dollar note from his wallet and set it on the counter beside her. 'You provided lunch and breakfast is in the box. I'll pay for tonight's dinner. Don't argue.'

It wasn't his quietly spoken words but the cool, steady gaze that accompanied them that warned her not to push him. Pick your battles and never use all your ammo in the opening salvo. Her father had taught her that too, bless his military soul. 'Okay,' she said with a cool and measuring gaze of her own. She picked up the fifty-dollar note and headed for the door. 'Good hamburgers heavy on the BBQ sauce requires local knowledge,' she said. 'I'll go ask the receptionist where we can find some.'

The receptionist, whose name, Erin discovered, was Delia, gave more than advice. She called the shop, placed their order, and arranged for it to be delivered to the room. Two works hamburgers, one with extra BBQ sauce, and an extra large serve of hot chips with chicken salt.

'Who are the chips for?' asked Erin.

'Your man. He looks hungry.'

Great. Another woman hell-bent on feeding him. 'He's not my man,' she said firmly. 'He's just a travelling companion. A chauffeur.'

Delia cackled. 'Honey, if that man's a chauffeur, I'll eat both your burgers *and* the chips.' And after a pause, 'Mind you, he'd look mighty fine in the uniform. Any uniform.'

'Yeah, well, thanks for that.' Erin did *not* want to picture Tristan Bennett in uniform. Unfortunately, she couldn't help it.

He looked fabulous. Cool, confident, heartbreakingly remote...

'Where were we?' said Delia.

'Uniforms,' she said wistfully. 'Navy formals. The dark blue with the gold braid.' She had no idea what the Interpol uniform looked like, so she'd gone with what she knew.

'I knew you'd catch on,' said the older woman. 'By the way, there's a twenty-minute wait on that order. Sol's always backed up this time of night.'

'I don't mind waiting.'

'Why would you when you have a man in uniform to think about?' said Delia. 'You can use the time to visualise just how you'd go about getting him out of it.'

Five minutes later Erin was back in the motel suite. The burgers were on their way, she told Tristan, eyeing him darkly before following up with the somewhat puzzling statement that she wasn't the slightest bit interested in the type of dress uniform Interpol cops wore. 'Not a problem,' he said and watched with no little amusement as she banged around in the kitchen, setting plates on the table, and searching the cupboards for wineglasses for the bottle of white she handed to him.

'We're drinking?' he asked.

'I am,' she said. 'I'm in need of a distraction.'

'From what?'

'You.'

'Care to expand on that?'

'Absolutely not,' she said, finally finding some wineglasses and setting them down on the table in front of him. 'Pour.'

He poured generously, for both of them. Maybe she had a point. Maybe wine would dull the senses and cloud the mind enough so that he could get through the night without doing anything monumentally stupid like acting on the awareness that lay thick and insistent between them. Or maybe not. 'What if the wine doesn't distract you?' he asked. 'What if it makes you even more focussed on what you're trying to avoid?'

'Let's not dwell on it,' she said, lifting her glass. 'To opals and the buying of them. To brilliant designs, worldwide recognition, and restraint when it comes to acting on impulse with men in uniform.'

'I don't wear a uniform,' he said.

'Not sure I needed to know that.'

Tristan shrugged, stifling his smile. 'To your success,' he said.

'Thanks.' She touched her glass to his and drank.

The food arrived some ten minutes later and although the burgers were good, the chips were better. 'Good idea,' he said, indicating the chips piled high on a plate between them.

'Delia's idea,' said Erin wryly. 'She thought you looked hungry.'

He was hungry. 'Who's Delia?'

'The receptionist.' Erin regarded him curiously. 'Women really like the thought of feeding you, don't they? Why is that?'

'It's some sort of nurturing instinct,' he said. 'Also the way to a man's heart. You should know this.'

'So has Delia captured your heart?'

'Not yet, but she's certainly in the running. These are good chips.'

'Anyone else cook for you back in England?'

He knew what she was asking. Thought it as good a time as any to let her know his thoughts on the subject. 'Not on a permanent basis.'

'How about a regular basis?'

'Not even that.'

'I don't feel an overwhelming need to feed you,' she said solemnly.

'No nurturing thoughts?'

'Not one.'

'This is a good thing,' he said.

She smiled. 'Nope, when I think of you it's all about wild passionate sex and losing my mind. I suspect you've heard that before.'

Not in this lifetime he hadn't. 'Don't you have any sense of self-preservation at all?' he demanded. Because his thoughts were already there, his body tense and hard as he undressed her in his mind, roughly, urgently, and took her right there in the kitchen. 'Dammit, Erin!' He closed his eyes, muttered a prayer, and tried to remember exactly why it was that he didn't want Erin Sinclair in his bed or anywhere else he could think of to take her.

Because she was dangerous, his brain reminded him. Whether she was gunning for his heart or not, Erin Sinclair had the power to reach out and engage him on every level he could think of and a few more he couldn't even name and he didn't want that. No, he couldn't risk that. He wouldn't. 'Drink your wine,' he commanded, burning up with the knowledge that if she pushed him, heaven forbid, if she even looked at him with an invitation in her eyes, he'd never be able to keep himself leashed.

'Good idea,' she said, and picked up her wineglass with hands that trembled ever so slightly. 'Geez. Who knew?'

Exactly.

'I think we need another distraction,' she said, setting her wineglass carefully back down on the table, and headed from the room without another word. When she returned she had her sketchbook in one hand and a fistful of pencils in the other.

'What are you doing?'

'Your portrait.'

'Why?'

'You, me, a sketchpad between us…' she said, setting it on her lap and using her knees as an easel. 'I'm going to objectify you.'

It sounded reasonable. 'Who taught you to draw?'

'My mother, at first. Then I took classes. It's a useful skill for any designer to have.' Her pencil moved sure and swift across the page. 'Brood for me.'

'Excuse me?'

'You know. Brood. Think about whatever it is that's bothering you.'

'You mean apart from the thought of wild, unfettered sex with a woman who doesn't want to feed me?'

'Not that,' she said quickly. 'You need to think about something other than that.'

'Not sure that's possible,' he muttered.

'Think about your work.'

Tristan glared at her.

'Perfect.'

Tristan glared at her some more. 'How long is this going to take?'

'Not that long. I'm almost done. This is a speed portrait. I only want the lines. The essence of you is something I'm trying to avoid.' She lifted her gaze from the paper and her pencil paused as if momentarily distracted. 'I have a piece of tiger-eye the exact colour of your eyes,' she said at length. 'If I set it in a ring for you, would you wear it?'

He doubted it.

'I was thinking of something like this.' She turned to a fresh page in her sketchbook, set it on the table, and the picture of a ring began to take shape. The design was simple: a wide band with a squarish insert of polished stone. With a few strokes of her pencil she managed to make it look both elegant and bold.

Tristan shrugged.

'Your enthusiasm overwhelms me,' she muttered, picking up her wineglass. 'I'll make it for you anyway, as payment for coming opal-hunting with me. I'm thinking white gold for the band. Platinum if I can get hold of it.'

'Are you always this generous with people you hardly know?'

'You give some, you get some.'

Tristan wanted some. Badly. And he didn't know how long he could hold off before he reached out and simply took. 'Erin—'

'I know,' she said breathlessly. 'You know, maybe this portrait business isn't such a good idea. Maybe I should go for a walk instead.' She stood abruptly and reached for his plate.

'Leave it.'

'Oh, boy.' She reached for her wine.

'Refill?' He reached for the bottle.

'No!' And then more calmly, 'Thank you. I'm going to take that walk now. Then I'm going to come back and take a shower and go to bed. Alone.'

'It's a good plan.' His voice was rough, strained, his control was close to non-existent. 'But if you're still here by the time I get these dishes to the sink, it's not going to happen. You and me naked on the table will happen, and then maybe, *maybe*, we'll make it to the shower. You know that, don't you?'

She nodded. Swallowed hard. 'I'm not quite sure I'm ready for that to happen.'

Neither was he. 'Enjoy your walk.' He stood up, reached for the dinner plates and took them to the counter. By the time he'd scraped the scraps into the bin she was gone.

What in hell was wrong with him? He never lost control when he was with a woman. Not ever. He hoped Erin's walk was a long one. He hoped she had the quickest shower in history and that she went to bed directly afterwards, just as she'd said. He would stay up late, watch some TV. And then, when she was safely tucked away for the night, sound asleep, and he'd watched all there was to watch on the television, and read all there was to read in the newspaper, when his mind was foggy with fatigue and his body was aching with tiredness, maybe then he'd think about going to bed.

CHAPTER FOUR

TRISTAN was dreaming of the dockyards of Prague and row upon row of shipping containers. They were slick with sea spray and shrouded in mist that twisted and eddied around his feet as he walked towards that last unopened container. Cars; he was looking for stolen cars; the permit to search was in his partner's pocket, and they were onto something. He could feel it in the air, see it in the eyes of passing dockyard workers.

Cars. Shiny, expensive, luxury cars, that was what they were looking for. The hour was late and he was tired, deathly tired, but there'd been something in Jago's voice when he'd talked about this latest container load that no one wanted to pick up that had had him breaking deep cover and calling it in. Jago was frightened; something had gone badly wrong. And scum like Jago didn't frighten easily.

'Tell me why we're doing this,' said Cal when he'd collected him and hightailed it down to the yards. 'Tell me why you just blew off months of undercover work on one lousy container load of stolen cars.'

He couldn't say. He didn't know. 'Something's wrong.'

'Yeah, your judgement. Seriously, man. We nearly had the whole damn lot of them, the entire cartel.'

'The big dogs bailed this morning. It's time.' It was past time.

Death. He could smell it as they drew closer and it made his hair stand on end. 'Has anyone checked the container?' he asked the night watchman who padded alongside him, grim and wary.

'Hell, no,' said the man. 'The men are spooked. You can see that for yourself.'

Not cars. Not just cars. He knew that as surely as he knew his own name, and all of a sudden he didn't want to open up that container, didn't want to know what was inside. 'We should wait for backup.'

'You going soft on me, old man?' This from Cal.

Not soft. But gut instinct had kept him alive too many times for him to ignore it, and right now instinct was telling him to stay the hell away from that container. 'I don't like it.'

'Hey, you're the one who dragged me out of bed and down here.' Cal reached the container and started sliding bars into their open position. Bars that had kept whatever was in that container in. The dockworkers of Prague had the right of it, but Cal couldn't feel it. Cal who was young and fearless and hadn't yet seen the things that Tristan had seen.

'Cal! Wait!'

But Cal hadn't waited. He'd thrown that door open and the smell had poured over them like a wave. Death. He should have called this in days ago, when the missing container had finally arrived. He'd known something was going down but he'd bided his time. Not just cars, no cars at all, just filth and mattresses and shapeless, nameless lumps and then he knew what this container had been trafficking and why the cartel had spooked when it hadn't come in on time. His eyes watered, he couldn't see for darkness, didn't want to see. 'Call the paramedics,' he said as Cal stumbled back, white-faced and clumsy with his need to get away. 'Some of them might still be alive.'

He should have called it in earlier. Three days ago, when the container had first hit the dock. He'd known something big had gone down, he just hadn't known what. So he'd waited.

And waited.

Erin woke to the echo of a noise reverberating in her head, not entirely sure if she'd been dreaming or if a sound really had woken her. She lay in the little single bed in the unfamiliar motel room, hardly breathing, just waiting. Waiting for what?

She didn't know.

Uneasiness came quickly, spreading over her like a blanket as the noise came again; a harsh, anguished cry of grief and desperation that was universally recognisable, never mind that it was wordless.

Tristan.

Erin hadn't been dreaming. But Tristan was.

What to do?

Her first instinct was to go to him, hold him, and let him take from her what comfort he could. Her second instinct was to feed him. Damn! She lay in bed, listening to him thrash about, and then the noise stopped abruptly and light crept into her room from the gap beneath the door. He was awake.

She heard his bedroom door open, heard him go into the bathroom and then there was the splash of running water and she figured he was dousing his face. She wanted to go to him then, and ask him what was troubling him, but she stayed where she was, motionless in her indecision. He wouldn't thank her for her interference. He'd close up tight, stare at her with eyes as fierce as any mountain cat and tell her that it was nothing, that he was fine, and that she should go back to bed.

Damned if he'd tell her anything. She knew the breed. Damned if he would.

She heard him turn the tap off, heard the click of a light switch as he turned the bathroom light off and padded quietly down the hallway.

He didn't turn his bedroom light off. She could picture him sitting on the bed with his elbows on his knees and his head in his hands and cursed him afresh for being what he was. For making her care that he was hurting.

She wanted to go to him. She desperately wanted to help him. And knew that she could not.

Maybe he was reading. She hoped that was what he was doing.

Or maybe he simply slept better these days with the light on.

CHAPTER FIVE

BREAKFAST the following morning was a subdued affair; never mind that the sun was shining and the prospect of hunting down the perfect opal loomed bright. Erin watched in silence as Tristan, freshly showered and shaved, slotted two bits of raisin bread into the toaster. He knew his way around a kitchen, that much was certain. The dishes from last night had been washed and stowed away, and the tea towel had been hung to dry. What was more, the bathroom was tidy too, not a toothpaste smear or a dropped towel in sight. Just the lingering scent of soap and man, and the memory of a cry in the darkness that she couldn't forget. 'Sleep well?' she asked casually.

'Fine,' he said. And after a moment, 'You?'

'Like a baby.'

'Good.' He nodded, waited for the toast to pop.

He wasn't going to tell her about his nightmare. Wasn't even going to acknowledge its existence. Her father and Rory were the same. Forever shutting her out and telling her everything was okay when, clearly, all hell had broken loose. Trying to protect her, she knew that. Trying to shield her from the darkness that came with war, and she appreciated their concern, she really did, but she resented it too. She was stronger than they gave her credit for. Strong enough to listen. Plenty strong enough to help.

Toast popped and Tristan slid the pieces onto a plate and slathered them with butter, before loading up the toaster again. 'Want some?' he offered, gesturing towards the plate.

Sighing, Erin took a piece. 'Coffee's hot,' she said by way of contribution to the breakfast cause. Given the night he'd just had she figured he was going to need a couple of cups before he'd be ready to seize the day. 'There's a one-man mine about forty kilometres north-east of here,' she said. 'I thought we might head out there first up this morning.'

'You don't need to phone ahead?'

Erin shook her head. 'Can't. Old Frank's not one for phones. The upside is that he does love his opals.' Another thought occurred to her. 'Er, he likes his guns too. You're not going to get all righteous about him having unlicensed firearms on the premises, are you?'

'Only if he's waving one of them in my face,' said Tristan.

This was a distinct possibility. Frank and his twenty-two tended to meet potential customers shortly after they pulled up on his plot. Mind you, that particular gun probably was licensed. 'Maybe you could wait in the car while I go and find him.'

'I don't think so.' Tristan's voice was implacable.

'Ooh, tough guy. Be still my beating heart.'

The tough guy favoured her with a look that could have frozen Sydney harbour and Erin sent him a sunny smile in return. She'd worry about who went and found Frank when they got there, she decided, because there was obviously no sense talking about it *now*. One thing was for certain, she thought smugly. Tristan wasn't thinking about whatever was giving him nightmares any more. No. He was thinking about ways to chain her to the car.

Tristan's eyes narrowed. 'I know that smile,' he said warningly. 'My sister has one just like it.'

'Really?' Erin's smile widened. 'More toast?'

An hour later they rolled onto Frank's patch of dirt, studiously ignoring the barrage of no-trespassing signs and the bone-white cow skull mounted on a stake by the front gate.

'Colourful,' said Tristan as he got out of the car and came to help her drag the broken-hinged farm gate closed behind them. 'How did you come across this place again?'

'Rory and I were out this way about two years back and stopped to help Frank with a busted radiator hose. Of course, we didn't know who he was back then, but we got to talking and one thing led to another.'

'I can imagine.'

'Next thing you know we're getting a tour of his mine and I'm sifting through a handful of rough-cut opal and doing business. I think it was fate.'

'Not horoscopes?'

'That too.' Erin scoured the desolate landscape in front of them and waved energetically in the general direction of the old silver caravan in the distance. 'I think he's home. I just saw a glint of sunlight on steel.'

'Where?'

'Over by the caravan.'

'Great,' said Tristan. 'Get in the car.'

She got in the driver's side, held out her hand for the keys, and when Tristan somewhat reluctantly handed them over she headed for the caravan.

'Do you think he'll remember you?' asked Tristan

'I'm pretty sure he will,' she said, with a nod of her head for good measure. Eventually.

Frank West did remember her. The grin on his sun-battered face and the lack of a twenty-two in his hands confirmed it. He didn't remember Tristan.

'Who's the muscle?' he wanted to know.

'Frank, this is Tristan. Tristan, meet Frank.'

Tristan nodded.

Frank eyed Tristan curiously. 'Seems a bit up-tight,' he said.

'We're working on it,' said Erin, and smothered a smile when Tristan sent her a glance that told her she could work on him forever; he still wasn't going to bend.

'Got me some nice black opal,' said Frank.

'Sorry, Frank. The budget won't run to the blacks.' There was a ten-thousand-dollar limit on the cost of materials for the competition pieces, to even the playing field. Anyone could make a million dollars' worth of Argyle diamonds look good. 'I'm after some rough-cut boulder opal.'

'Got some good quality blues,' he said. 'What shape?'

'Freeform.'

Frank's eyes brightened considerably. Free-form was a harder sell than the more common oval and square shapes. 'Better come into the office,' he said, and sat them down at the table in the little silver caravan that doubled as both living quarters and business premises. 'Sure you don't want to take a look at the blacks?'

'Bring them out by all means,' she said with a grin, 'but unless you have any for sale under two thousand, all I'm going to do is admire them.'

Frank sighed and turned his attention to a row of opal-filled jam jars high up on a shelf. He bypassed the first half a dozen jam jars on the ledge in favour of a selection from further along, eventually taking down three jars and setting them on the table. He opened one up, and poured the contents carefully onto the table. 'Homebrew?' he asked Tristan. 'I figure you're going to need it before she's through.'

'Go ahead,' murmured Erin as she started sorting through the opals, piece by piece. 'This could take a while.'

'She was here for three hours last time she came,' said Frank.

'*How* long?' said Tristan.

'I figure that's a yes,' said Frank and opened the fridge door to reveal a tub of margarine, half a tomato, a row of empty beer glasses where the milk should be, and a twenty litre steel keg, complete with tap. He filled three glasses with beer from the keg, one for each of them, and took a seat.

'How long do you think she'll take this time?' asked Tristan.

'I've gotten smarter in my old age, see? That there first jar is to help her get her eye in. It's a practice jar, so to speak, to remind her what she's not looking for.'

'Gee, thanks, Frank,' said Erin, not bothering to look up from the opals she was sorting. 'What's in the second jar?'

'You'll find some nice opal in the second.'

'And the third?' asked Tristan.

'My best boulder pieces. She'll find what she's looking for in the third.'

'Why not give her the third jar first?' said Tristan.

Frank eyed him pityingly. 'You don't know much about women, do you, son?'

Tristan sighed, and reached for his beer.

'Would *you* like to see some black opal?' Frank asked Tristan speculatively. 'Got a stone there that'd make a fine engagement ring for a non-traditional kind of woman.'

Tristan froze with his beer halfway to his lips and Erin sniggered. 'Frank, you're scaring him.'

'A man needs to contemplate the future every now and then,' said Frank with a toothless grin as he headed past a curtain of faded blue cloth and into the bedroom section of the caravan. He came back with a small roll of red velvet cradled gently in the crook of his arm and Erin sighed and abandoned the opals on the table in favour of scooting over, closer to Tristan. Frank was determined to show off his blacks to someone and it was useless to pretend she wasn't interested.

There was a fortune in opals nestling on that there red velvet strip, she thought in awe as the old miner unrolled his best onto the table in front of him. Enough to buy Frank a mansion if he wanted one. Five mansions.

'This here's the latest,' said Frank proudly, turning over an opal the size of a twenty-cent piece. It was turquoise on black, shot through with yellow and a brilliant fiery red. 'Haven't seen colour like that in thirty years. Not since old Fisty dug up the Sorcerer's Stone and you know what happened to that.'

Tristan didn't.

'It vanished,' said Frank. 'Disappeared into thin air. One minute it was there on its pedestal and the next minute…*poof*. Gone! Saw it happen with my own eyes. That's why I never put my stones on display under glass. They don't like it. They disappear.'

'Someone could have taken it,' said Tristan mildly.

'That there room was locked down tighter than a Russian submarine the minute it disappeared, and everyone in the room was body-searched. Nothing!'

'Maybe someone swallowed it,' said Tristan.

'It was the size of a tennis ball.'

'Or hid it.'

'In that room?' Frank shook his head. 'It was one of them contemporary museums. You couldn't hide dust in that place.'

'Which museum was that?' asked Tristan and Erin lifted her gaze from the opals to stare at him with amused exasperation. His interest in the opals set out in front of him was cursory. His interest in Frank's story was all-encompassing. 'You can't help yourself, can you?'

'What?' he said.

'Doing the cop thing. Aren't you supposed to be on leave?'

'I am on leave.'

'Yet you're sitting here asking questions about a legendary fire opal that's been missing for, what, twenty years?'

'More like thirty,' said Frank.

'Just curious,' said Tristan.

'You were working it,' she said sternly. 'Trying to solve a thirty-year-old crime in your spare time.'

'Don't you have boulder opal to look at?' he countered.

'I'll get back to them eventually.' Just as soon as she'd finished ogling the blacks and making her point. 'You know what your problem is? You've lost your balance. You're all work.'

'Really?' said Tristan coolly.

'Yes, really.' Erin stood her ground. 'You've been so busy chasing villains that you've forgotten how to chase rainbows.'

'I know perfectly well how to chase rainbows,' he said.

'Oh, yeah? When was the last time you acted on impulse? When was the last time you let whimsy have its way?'

Tristan's eyes lightened as he sent her a lopsided smile she couldn't even begin to resist. 'I'm here, aren't I?'

Erin found the perfect opal pieces in the third jar she looked in, just as Frank had predicted. There were three of them altogether. Two halves of the same opal, expertly cut into slim columns of shimmering blues and greens and perfect for earrings. The third piece showed similar colour and form; only this one had a thin streak of potch running through it like a silvery grey river. This one would form the basis of the necklace, she decided, never mind its irregularity, and when Frank named a price that was more than reasonable, she was decided.

'There's better than that in there,' he said bluntly.

'I know…' Erin picked up the stone and held it up to the light, turning it this way and that. 'But the colour's exquisite and there's just something about it.' She paid cash for the stones and stood just inside the caravan door, rubbing the opal between her fingers as she watched Tristan wander over towards a rusty old ute that Frank seemed to be using as a storage cupboard. There was something about Tristan too. An almost irresistible blend of vulnerability and strength that called to her, even as she railed against it. 'I know it'll be a challenge,' she said absently, 'but that's the one I want.'

'Women,' muttered Frank, and Erin tore her gaze away from Tristan to raise an eyebrow in silent query.

'You give that boy some room to move, y'hear? It don't always help to have a woman pointing out the obvious. Sometimes a man needs to solve things his own way, and in his own good time.'

'What if his way's not working,' she countered, thinking of Tristan's nightmare.

'Then ya gotta get sneaky.'

'You mean subtle.'

'Subtle. Sneaky. Never could tell the difference, between the two.'

'It's a good thing we women can tell the difference then, isn't it?'

Frank snorted, handed her a plastic Ziploc bag to put the opals in and with the deal done they headed over towards Tristan, still standing there eyeing the ute.

'It's a thirty-nine Ford,' said Tristan.

'Bought that old girl from a broke miner for a hundred dollars,' said Frank. 'Look at the lines on her!'

Tristan was looking. 'Is it for sale?'

'Depends what you wanted to do with her,' said Frank. 'I wouldn't sell her to just anyone.'

'I want to restore it,' said Tristan. 'I'll give you six hundred for it.'

'Twelve hundred,' said Frank.

'There's a lot of rust,' said Tristan.

'Surface rust,' said Frank.

Surface rust? Erin bent down and picked at a flake of it with her index finger and stifled a giggle as it fell to the ground leaving a hole the size of a twenty-cent piece.

'Five hundred,' said Tristan, and Erin stared from the rusted wreck to Tristan in bemusement. The man lived in England. In London. In an apartment. What on earth was he going to do with a thirty-nine Ford ute?

'Does it run?' she asked as Frank wrestled with the bonnet to reveal one of the biggest engines she'd ever seen.

'Had her purring like a kitten fifteen years ago.'

'Yes, but does it purr now?'

'Four hundred,' said Tristan as he worked his way around the old engine. 'Know anyone who could get her to Sydney for me?'

'That'll cost you an extra two hundred,' said Frank. 'Six-fifty all up should about cover it.'

'Done,' said Tristan, and shaking hands with Frank, became the proud owner of a rusty paddock junker.

'What are you going to do with it after you've restored it?' she asked him. 'Have it shipped over to

London?' By the time he'd finished restoring and transporting it, the old heap would have cost him a fortune.

Tristan shrugged. 'I haven't really thought about it.'

'That's ridiculous!'

'No,' he said, the ghost of a smile hovering around his lips. 'It's a rainbow.'

They visited three more opal mines after that, two of them on Frank's recommendation, and Tristan suffered the shopping in stoic silence. He didn't rush her, distract her, or try to influence her. If it took an hour to sort through a tinful of boulder opals, then that was what it took. Cops obviously acquired a lot of patience in the course of their work, Erin decided approvingly. Rory's would have run out around midday.

It was after five by the time they reached the motel and Erin was no richer for opal than she had been when they'd left Frank's. Not that it mattered. She had three pieces; three extraordinary pieces of opal and the jewellery that would come of them would be stunning. As far as opal-buying was concerned, she was done.

'We won't be needing that third night after all,' she told Delia, when they stopped by reception on the way back to their rooms. 'We'll head off in the morning.'

'Checkout's at eleven,' said Delia, eyeballing them both. 'You look spent. You need to go and have a soak in the hot pool. Here.' She reached beneath the counter and came up with a small gold-coloured entry coin. 'A two-night stay'll get you a single entry into the pool complex. Try it.'

'I didn't bring any bathers,' said Erin, turning to Tristan. 'Did you?'

'No.'

Delia's eyes brightened. 'Of course, there's always the secret pools hereabouts. The ones we don't tell the tourists about. You can skinny-dip in those.'

Skinny-dip? As in get naked with Tristan Bennett in an isolated hot pool? Erin didn't think so. But Delia was insistent.

'Here.' She found a map for them and marked it with an X. 'It's quite the picture, especially at sunset. I dare say you'll have the place to yourselves.'

'No,' said Erin, shaking her head. She'd made it through the entire day without letting the sexual tension escalate. For dinner she was thinking the bowling club, carvery food, plenty of people and lots of noise. She was into awareness expulsion, not isolated hot pools at sunset.

'I could swim,' said Tristan, with a lazy smile that was pure challenge. The smile had Delia fanning herself with a tourist brochure. She fanned Erin too.

'Relax,' said Delia. 'Go for a swim.' And with a chuckle, 'Don't forget to breathe.'

The hot pool didn't look particularly inviting from a distance. Someone had gone to the trouble of bringing in a few flat rocks and scattering them around the edge of the pool but otherwise it was as bleak as nature could make it. A scattering of stunted greenery, miles and miles of flat grey ground and a sun that looked like a fireball about to ram into the horizon. 'I'm not sure why the locals feel the need to keep this one a secret,' muttered Erin as she stepped from the car.

'It has a certain elemental appeal,' said Tristan from

the other side of the car, door open as he stood there surveying the landscape. 'Water looks good.'

'Yeah.' Pity about the thin film of grey-brown clay that covered everything, including the surface of the water. A desert oasis it wasn't. Maybe if she closed her eyes she could rearrange reality and *pretend* it was a desert oasis. Add a few palm trees, white sand instead of the superfine clay beneath her feet. There, much better. She opened her eyes to find a shirtless Tristan just about to shed his trousers. Definitely *not* on her list of oasis improvements. 'Er, we're not really planning to skinny-dip, are we?' she asked, eyeing his trousers with equal measures of what she was pretty sure were lust and apprehension.

'I'm easy,' he said.

That he wasn't. Not even in her imagination. In her imagination, he was a wild and reckless lover, chasing pleasure, and taking it, with breathtaking intensity. 'Underwear needs to stay on,' she said firmly.

Tristan shrugged and moments later he'd stripped down to boxers and was in the pool and heading for the far side of it, explorer-style. Men! So much for sitting back and rejuvenating the mind while the water washed away the dirt of the day. Sighing, Erin stripped down to her black cotton panties and matching singlet and waded into the pool. The water temperature was just short of hot, and if she discounted the squish factor of the clay beneath her feet and not being able to see what was on the bottom, it was really quite pleasant. The water got deeper fast and Erin pushed off and swam lazily to the middle of the pool before turning onto her back and floating. 'I'm picturing myself in a desert oasis,' she murmured as Tristan appeared at her side.

'You are in a desert oasis,' he said mildly. 'This is great.'

'You wouldn't understand.'

He regarded her with a tilt to his lips that she tried to ignore. 'Are you alone at this desert oasis?'

'No, there's a waiter. He looks a lot like you.'

'Tell him to swat that mosquito next to your ear. It's the size of a bus.'

'I would,' she said, waving away the mosquito herself, 'But he's busy seeing to the horses.'

'Horses? What kind of horses?'

'A fiery black stallion and a dainty white mare. The stallion's my ride.'

'You should reconsider,' said Tristan lazily. 'That horse is far too powerful for you. Some things are best left to men.'

'I can handle him.'

'Don't say I didn't warn you.' He sighed and sank below the surface, reappearing moments later. 'Don't suppose your waiter has a cold beer handy?'

'Good idea. I'll get him to bring two.' She rolled over and swam towards the side of the pool. 'Hey, there's a ledge to stand on.'

'Handy,' said Tristan, coming to join her on it.

She shifted over to give him some room, lots of room. Lucky for her it was a long ledge. She closed her eyes and concentrated hard on ignoring the effect a superbly muscled Tristan was having on her senses.

'Erin?' he murmured, his voice sliding over her like a caress.

'What?' Breathe in. Breathe out.

'Open your eyes and turn around. Slowly.'

Erin's eyes snapped open and she eyed him anxiously. 'What is it? It's not a snake, is it?' She wasn't fond of snakes.

'No.'

'Goanna?' She wasn't exactly fond of goannas either. Something about those razor-sharp claws.

'No.'

'Emu?' Now emus she liked.

'Turn around. You're missing the sunset.'

Oh. The sunset. At the secluded hot pool. With Tristan.

With as much indifference as she could muster, Erin turned around.

The sky was ablaze with colour. Fiery oranges, and reds streaked with indigo, and a smattering of wispy grey cloud. Not your typical tropical island sunset, nothing like it, she thought in awe. This sky was all about power and raw, undiluted glory over an earth that was stark and barren. It was primitive and overwhelming and it slammed into her like a fist, daring her to be as bold when it came to living her life and making the most of the moments she was given. Like now, beneath a cinnamon sky at a secluded oasis. With a man she couldn't even look at without wanting. And wondering what it would take to chase the shadows from his eyes.

She sank beneath the surface, searching for answers and some sort of direction and surfaced instead with a handful of mud. 'Tristan?'

He looked at her in silent query, so solemn and restrained that it made her heart bleed. And then…

Splat!

The mud hit him square in the shoulder and Erin was racing towards the edge of the pool in search of more accessible ammunition, laughing helplessly at his astonishment. 'People pay good money to be covered in this stuff. Honest, it's supposed to have healing powers.'

'Well, hell. Why didn't you say so earlier?'

Splattt! His aim was good; his hands were large. One strike and she was all but covered in the stuff and still she laughed as she reached the shallows and tried, unsuccessfully, to nail him again. She turned sideways and crouched low in response to his next volley, flinging mud over her shoulder at random; outmanned, outgunned, but in no way outmanoeuvred as she disappeared beneath the water only to be snagged by the ankle and brought up spluttering, chest to chest with an amused and muddy Tristan. The sun was behind him, accentuating his darkness, but the shadows in his eyes had gone. 'Hey, it works! You're almost smiling.' She was almost whimpering as her hands slid to his shoulders, finding sinew and muscle beneath mud-slicked skin. 'Maybe we should bottle some. Bring it along for the ride.'

'Can the oasis come too? Because I really don't think the mud's going to work without it.' His eyes were darkening as he spoke, the amusement fading, replaced by something a whole lot more intense. Not shadows, not yet, but a flame of something that licked over her, licked over them both, and set her heart to hammering.

Be bold, she thought as his eyes grew heavy with intent and his hand brushed the curve of her cheek and slid to the curve of her neck as he drew her closer. And then his lips were on hers, soft and coaxing, and she wasn't thinking at all because the fire in the sky was in her as well, burning her up from the inside as she melted in his embrace.

She sought the wildness in him and found it. Tasted it on his tongue, felt it in his touch as he dragged her closer until there was nothing between them but the thin cotton of her singlet, her panties, and his boxers, and it was still too much to have between them and Tristan was in full agreement. Her top went, and then his hands were on her, rough and urgent, but his lips were in her hair, the curve of her neck, the hollow at her throat, and his lips were gentle.

'I thought you said you weren't ready for this,' he muttered.

'That was yesterday.' His hands were at her hips, anchoring her against his hardness, and it was exactly where she wanted to be, exactly what she needed, and then his hands moved lower, positioning her against him more fully as he surged against her. More. She sought it. Found it in the slickness of his skin, in the slide of that hard, muscled body beneath her hands, and then her hands were in his hair and she was offering him everything she was, everything she had to give.

He groaned, deep in his throat, and shuddered hard. There was no gentleness in the arm that snaked round her waist like a steel band, binding her to him while his other hand came up to cup her breast. Nothing gentle about that rough, urgent hand at her breast, kneading and teasing with ruthless skill. She wanted more, wanted his mouth on her skin, and she nipped at him to break their kiss, and dragged his head lower.

He couldn't get enough of her, of the sleek feminine curves beneath his palm. Couldn't get enough of her flavour, her flesh, and she was with him every step of the way; he could feel it in the hard little tremors that ripped through her body, hear it in the mindless whimper he drew from her as he devoured her breast with his lips.

He wanted to stop. He desperately wanted her to do something or say something that would make him stop before he drowned in her, drowned them both, but passion held sway here now; passion and raw, unfettered need and it was merciless.

He wanted her naked, couldn't see how to get her that way without drawing away from her and that was impossible. 'Stop me,' he muttered. 'For God's sake, Erin, make me stop.'

'No.' As she wrapped her legs around his waist and water swirled around them and the sky caught fire.

There was nothing gentle about the kiss that followed. It was mindless and brutal and it was all that mattered. Nothing but this man and this moment and she matched him, need for violent, desperate need while the pleasure built and built. He was all darkness and greed and he was all she'd ever wanted. Everything she'd never wanted. Too strong, too wounded.

Too much.

She hesitated, just for an instant, wondering what she'd done, what she was doing, and he felt her withdrawal, he must have done, because the hands that held her so tightly released her. He broke their kiss and pushed her away to stare down at her with eyes full of anger, frustration, and a hint of pain that nearly destroyed her. He uttered a harsh, one-word expletive and turned away.

Not what a woman hoped to see in a man after the most intense sexual experience of her life.

'I'm sorry,' he said gruffly.

Not what she wanted to hear.

'I was rough on you. I lost control. There's no excuse for that.'

'I didn't mind,' she said, trying desperately to break down walls as fast as he built them. 'I liked what you did to me. I liked it when you lost control.'

He speared her with a glance. 'I didn't.'

She could see that.

'I didn't hurt you, did I?'

'No. Tristan—' What could a woman say to a man who was hell-bent on re-establishing his emotional and physical distance? 'I'm fine. Don't worry about me.' She didn't want his guilt. There was no need for it. No reason he should carry it. 'What do you normally do?' she said, with a tentative smile. 'After you've kissed a woman and she's melted in a puddle at your feet.'

'I'm not normally in a hot pool,' he said.

'Wing it.'

'I might dry off,' he said, his eyes lightening, just a little. 'I might bring her a towel so that she can dry off too.'

'That would be a good start.'

'Then I might find her that beer she was after on the way home. Or wine. Whatever she wanted.'

'I'm really liking where your head's at.'

He smiled at that, really smiled, and Erin bit back a sigh of relief. She didn't want his apology for what they'd just shared. Didn't want him to stew and to brood over something that neither of them had been able to control. 'It's not such a big thing, you and I and a couple of kisses.' She was lying through her teeth.

'You don't want to know where all this is heading?'

'No.' She was heading for heartbreak, she knew that much already. One step at a time.

CHAPTER SIX

TRISTAN was in turmoil. He didn't know what to think. Damn sure he didn't know what to say to the woman who'd just destroyed him with her kisses and then blocked his retreat with nothing more than clever words and a warm smile. He was used to keeping people out. Never revealing too much, never caring too much, always staying in control. His work demanded it, and when it came to his private life *he* demanded it.

He never lost control when he was with a woman. Not ever. He certainly didn't ravage them beneath a blood red sky with no thought of tenderness or care. No thought at all, truth be told, beyond sheer animal need.

He didn't want it. Didn't want Erin Sinclair filling needs he'd never known he had and leaving memories that would haunt him for the rest of his life. Erin in his arms, lost to everything but sensation, and the only thing that saved him from complete self-loathing was the knowledge that she'd been as much at the mercy of their love-making as he had. That she'd wanted him as mindlessly as he'd wanted her.

She just handled the afterwards a hell of a lot better.

So he would follow her lead and be an adult in the aftermath of near catastrophe. Nothing he didn't want to give, but he could show her some tenderness, he could do that. He could be civil and buy her a meal and act the gentleman.

It was the least she deserved.

He bought beer on the way back to the motel, and Chinese take-away to go with it, and she didn't object to him paying, not by so much as a glance. She hadn't objected to him doing the driving either. She was reading him, he thought grimly. Reading his need for some small measure of control with disturbing accuracy.

They ate back at the motel, in the little kitchenette, and he worked hard to make the evening almost normal and the conversation almost easy. It was the little things that tripped him up. Her delight at the spicy heat of the Mongolian lamb, never mind that her eyes were watering. Her unabashed appreciation for a cold beer straight from the bottle. The way she moved, the way she smiled. She was sensualist; he'd known that from the start. From the moment he'd kissed her in the driveway outside her mother's house, and vowed to stay away from her.

'So where to next?' he asked when they'd eaten their fill and cleared away the plates, and even that small domesticity carried with it an intimacy he didn't want. 'Inverell for sapphires?'

'In the morning.' She regarded him steadily. 'You don't have to come with me, you know. You could head back to Sydney tomorrow if you'd prefer.' Her lips curved into a slight smile. 'You could drive your ute home. You'd cut quite the dashing picture. Very James Dean.'

'James Dean drove a nineteen-fifty-five silver Porsche Spyder. I'm not quite seeing a connection between him in that and me heading down the highway in Frank's old Ford.'

'You'd probably have to be female to see that particular connection,' she said dryly. 'You men are far too literal. My point is that there are plenty of ways to get back to Sydney from here if you have a mind to.'

She was giving him an out, but damned if he was going to take it. Damned if he'd let her see how much she affected him. 'You still need sapphires for your competition pieces, don't you?'

'Yes, but if you're not comfortable—'

'Don't,' he said curtly. 'Just…don't.'

She nodded once and looked away. 'Two more days ought to do it.'

And two more nights. He didn't know what to do with himself, with all this time between now and morning. There was too much Erin in it.

'I thought I might work on some designs,' she said as she hung the tea towel to dry. 'Now that I have the opals.'

'I might take a walk into town.' She was the one who'd taken a walk last night. It seemed only fair that he be the one to do the walking tonight. 'I could be a while.' He might find a game of eight ball somewhere, or better still a rumble. Pity Luke wasn't here. Luke was always on for an argument involving fists. Or Pete. Two against one. Just enough to take the edge off his hunger for Erin, and if that didn't work there was always Jake.

Nobody messed with Jake.

He was halfway to town when he took it in his head to call his oldest brother. In Singapore.

'You in trouble?' said Jake, the minute he'd said hello.

'No.' *Yes.* 'I'm in Lightning Ridge.' Playing body-guard to three opals and a beautiful woman whose body he wanted with a ferocity that left him aching.

'And?' said Jake.

'And what?'

'Ask me how I am and I'm likely to strangle you.'

'There's a woman.'

Dead silence at that, and then, 'Is she a criminal?'

'No.'

'Psychopath?'

'No.'

'Married but nonetheless pregnant with your child?'

'No.'

'I'm not seeing a downside here. You're going to have to help me out. Have you slept with her yet?'

'No.'

More silence. A long, long silence, after which Jake sighed heavily. 'Dammit, Tris. Please tell me you're not calling for advice about women. Call Pete. He's always in love.'

And never in love. 'She's in my head.'

'This is bad,' said Jake. 'You need to get her out of there immediately. You need to head butt something.'

Typical martial arts solution. 'There's the telegraph pole.'

'Perfect. You'll feel much better afterwards. Call me from the hospital.'

'I was wondering,' he said doggedly, 'if you ever managed to get Jianna out of your head.' They'd never talked about Jake's ill-fated marriage, not once. He'd never known how.

'You want my advice? All right, then, you've got it. Walk away. Stay away.'

'You haven't answered my question.'

'You don't want to hear my answer to that question.'

'I think I do,' he said quietly.

He didn't think his brother was going to answer. He'd pushed too far. And then Jake spoke.

'You want to know if I still bleed? If I still think of Ji every day and dream of her at night? The answer's no.' And with a dark and biting humour, 'Sometimes I go days without thinking of her at all.'

Tristan was dreaming of the dockyards of Prague and a decision he'd taken too long to make. Again.

He woke in a lather of sweat and a tangle of sheets, with his heart thudding in his chest and his soul full of bile. He shoved the sheet aside, flicked the bedside lamp on, and sat there on the side of the bed, breathing hard. When was he ever going to make peace with these memories? How was he ever going to shake them loose?

They'd said it wasn't his fault. That he'd played it by the book, and that much was true. He'd played it straight down the line, both the undercover work and the takedown. He hadn't known what was in that container, he couldn't have known. And still the nightmares came.

A shower would help, he thought wearily, and with

his next breath wondered if taking a shower at this time of the morning would wake Erin. No. The shower was adjacent to his room, not hers. He would be quiet. He would sluice away the sweat and the memories and by the time he was clean he'd have thought of something else to do with the rest of this night.

The water was hot but the spray was weak and he stood there beneath it, wishing it were fiercer while his heartbeat steadied and he shoved those memories back in their box. By the time he'd tugged on a pair of track pants and padded downstairs he was almost back in control. He headed towards the kitchen for something to eat, belatedly wondering why the light was on. He'd been the last to bed and he'd turned that light off; he could have sworn he'd turned it off.

He had. Someone else had turned it back on.

'Morning,' said Erin, abandoning her latest design in favour of taking a good long look at Tristan. He looked tired, she thought. Defeated. His demons were riding him hard.

'What are you doing here?' he said abruptly.

Not exactly the warmest of greetings, but then, she hadn't expected one. 'I had some designs I wanted to get down on paper,' she said by way of explanation, and it was true to a point. She *had* been working on her designs. But she'd been waiting for Tristan.

He looked at the drawings, looked at her. 'At four-thirty a.m.?'

She shrugged. 'Why not? I was awake.'

'I'm sorry if I woke you,' he said awkwardly, and she bled for him even as she cursed his reticence.

'Kettle's boiled,' she said, indicating the cup of hot tea in front of her. 'And last night's leftovers are in the oven.'

'You're feeding me?'

'Not at all.'

'Are you sure?' he muttered. 'It feels like you're feeding me.'

'I didn't cook it so it doesn't count.' Tristan's hair was tousled, he was shirtless again, and she tried to ignore the quickening of her blood and the warmth that blossomed low in her belly when she looked at him. She knew the feel of him now, knew it and craved it, but she wasn't out to seduce him. She wanted to help him. 'Do you have them every night?'

'Showers?'

'Nightmares.'

His silence spoke volumes.

'You want to talk about it?'

'No.'

'Ever heard the one about problems shared?'

'I've heard it,' he said. 'I just don't hold to it.'

Erin smiled ruefully. 'Yeah, well, maybe that's your problem.' She'd been expecting him to shut her out. She was used to it and not just from him. From her father. From Rory… Talking through their troubles wasn't an option and it wasn't just a gender thing. It was a warrior thing. 'Tough guy.'

'Not even close.'

So vulnerable, she thought with a catch in her throat. So heartbreakingly defiant as he stood there like some dark angel and dared her to breach his defences. His demons were his own; he would not share them. And still she tried to reach him. She was a warrior's daughter; she could do nothing less. 'Any ideas on how to make those nightmares go away?'

He reached for a glass, filled it with tap water and drank deeply. Stonewalling her deliberately, she thought with a sigh.

'I'm thinking of handing in my resignation,' he said gruffly. 'Finding another job.'

Erin blinked and leaned back in her chair. Not what she'd expected to hear. And *not* what she thought would help him, for all that the notion appealed mightily to *her*. 'Do you really think that's going to help?'

Tristan shrugged. 'Maybe.'

'What would you do?'

'I don't know.'

'What about internal transfer options?'

'Desk jobs,' he muttered.

'No one works on the frontline for ever,' she said carefully. 'How long have you been there?'

Silence.

Too long, she thought as she stood and headed towards the oven, hoping that the aroma pervading the room meant that the food was hot enough to serve because it was either feed him or take him in her arms and soothe his hurt in a different way. 'I think it's ready,' she said as she took the dishes from the oven.

'Are you sure you're not feeding me?'

'Don't dwell on it.'

'What if I put the food on the plates?' he said. 'That might help.'

Only to make her want him more. But she let him do

it anyway, careful to keep some distance between them as she picked up her loaded plate and took it to the table. Food was good. Food occupied hands that could otherwise be engaged in touching and caressing. 'Are you planning on getting any more sleep tonight?' she asked him between mouthfuls of lukewarm fried rice.

'No.'

'And we're done talking about work options?'

'If there's a God.'

She ignored his fervour and concentrated on the big picture. Eating would take all of ten minutes. After that it'd be her, Tristan, a motel suite, and three empty beds. 'The thing is, I'm experiencing a powerful need to help you take your mind off your troubles,' she confessed. 'I have a couple of options I think you might be interested in.'

'I'm listening,' he said.

'We pack up and drive. Move on. Men like running from their problems.'

Tristan ignored the jibe. His thoughts had taken a sensual turn as he imagined another way in which Erin might think of to ease his troubled mind. A timeless, instinctive way. 'What's the second option?'

'Of course, we'd have to backtrack a bit.'

He was already there. Back at the hot pool, right where they'd left off. With Erin in his arms and a fire in his blood.

'I don't suppose you'd like to go rock climbing?'

·

CHAPTER SEVEN

'GOOD thing we didn't take the climbing option,' said Erin some two hours later as they drove towards Inverell. She was in the passenger seat, bright-eyed and clearly in the mood for conversation, which suited Tristan just fine. He wasn't against small talk as such. Just so long as he didn't have to provide it.

'I was thinking Cornerstone Rib because it's a brilliant climb no matter how experienced you are,' she continued. 'But it's a two hour walk-in from the closest car park and over two hundred metres of vertical. Then there's the descent. It can get slippery in the rain, and Lord knows it's raining now.'

This was true. Wind whipped at the car and the wipers struggled to keep water off the windscreen. The weather had turned mean. 'What else do you do in your spare time?' he asked her as he checked to see if the windscreen wipers could go any faster. They couldn't.

'You mean besides scale vertical crags and drive thousands of miles in search of gemstones?' She paused to consider. 'Movies are good. And Rory's talking about rally-car driving. That could be fun. Matter of fact that might be something you should consider. Some sort of car racing.'

He'd considered it. For a few years there he'd considered nothing else, but in the end he'd gone a different way. 'You mean as a vocation?'

'I mean as a sport. Something simple to take the edge off the stress that comes with your real work.'

'You think car racing is simple?'

'Well, yeah.' She slid him an impish smile. 'You get in a car, you drive very fast and you win. How hard can it be?'

'Harder than that,' he said dryly.

'All the better,' she said cheerfully. 'Seriously, you need to find a way to relax. Maybe you could go to the raceway when we get back to Sydney. Take a test drive or something.'

'Let me get this straight. You're against the armed forces—and policing for that matter—because of the dangers involved but you encourage mountaineering and motor sports? I don't get it.'

'I'm not against someone choosing a dangerous occupation for a living,' she said loftily. 'I'm against secrecy, the tyranny of distance, and putting duty to country or mankind before family.'

'You don't think duty to country or mankind is important?'

'I didn't say that. Someone's got to do it. I appreciate that.'

'Just not *your* someone.'

'Exactly. And don't you look at me like that. I gave at the office.'

And every step of the way throughout her childhood, he thought, remembering her seafaring father. He *knew* how much the absence of a parent could colour a lifetime, knew that the scars she carried were real for all that they were internal. 'I'm not looking at you like that,' he said gently.

'And don't you pity me either!'

No. It would be a mistake to do that. But he did think he'd just gained a slightly deeper understanding of her. 'So what kind of someone are you looking for?'

'One who loves me and isn't afraid to admit it.'

Ouch. 'Besides that.'

'One who's in our relationship for the long haul,' she said next. 'I want laughter, even if it's sometimes mixed with tears. I want a lifetime of it.'

'What if it's not working out?'

'Then we both give a little more, bend a little more, and we make it work out.'

'What about money?'

'Money is good but it's optional. Workaholics need not apply. I can contribute to moneymaking endeavours.'

'What about military men? Can they apply?'

'No. Their passion for their work is admirable and they have many fine qualities but the cost to their families is unacceptable. I won't be shut out,' she said fiercely. 'I refuse to be.'

'Even if it's for your own good?'

'Do I look like a powder-puff to you? Do I look like I need protecting?'

He slid her a sideways glance. 'Yes.'

'Excuse me?' Her eyes narrowed and if she hadn't been sitting in the passenger seat he was pretty sure her

hands would have gone to her hips. 'This is a size thing, isn't it?'

'No.' It was far more complicated than that. 'It's an instinctive thing. Men protect what they cherish.'

'And women nurture what they love!'

'I think this is where the "give and take" philosophy comes into play,' he said dryly.

Erin scowled. 'Yeah, well, there's a lot to be said for a passionate, no-strings-attached and extremely short-lived love affair these days too.'

'Hell!' He rounded a curve at speed, overcorrected, and the car almost ended up in a ditch. 'Can Interpol cops apply for those?'

It was mid-afternoon before they reached Inverell. The streets were wide country thoroughfares and the architecture of the older buildings was early colonial, but the rest of it was a mixture of modern architectural styles and the city centre was armed with every convenience. Built on the back of sapphire-mining and agriculture, Inverell had grown big enough to hold its own.

Choosing a motel was harder this time but eventually Tristan pulled into the one deemed most suitable by them both; the one with undercover parking next to the reception area and carports next to each room.

'We need a couple of rooms for the night,' Erin told the young girl behind the reception desk as she ran her hands up and down her arms. It was cold in Inverell. Far colder than in Lightning Ridge.

'Adjoining?'

'Er…' Erin slid him a sideways glance.

'Separate,' he said. He couldn't do another night that close to Erin and not take her. He knew he couldn't. And for all her fast talk of a passionate, no strings attached and extremely short-lived love affair, he knew damn well that it wouldn't satisfy her. When Erin Sinclair gave, she gave everything. She deserved a man who could give something back.

'Rooms number eighteen and nineteen are free,' said the girl, 'and you won't get soaked bringing your stuff in.' She reached to one side for the keys as Erin filled in the paperwork. Tristan busied himself by picking up a brochure on sapphire mines in the area. He still didn't like it that she was paying for the accommodation. 'Are you interested in sapphires?' asked the girl as she turned back around and handed him a key, placing the other one on the bench next to Erin. 'We have some very reputable mining operations hereabouts. Here,' she said, picking up a flyer and handing it to him. 'This one's open today and they're having a sale.'

'Why the sale?' he asked.

'No idea,' she said. 'They're just having one.'

'What are the regular prices like?' asked Erin.

'It's popular with locals; that's always a good sign,' said the girl with a grin. 'I got my engagement ring there.' She held out her hand to show them the ring.

'It's lovely,' said Erin, leaning forward to examine it more closely even as Tristan took a hearty step back. 'Congratulations on your engagement.'

The girl beamed. 'We didn't want to spend much cause we're saving for a house, but I wanted something I could look at in fifty years time and still love as much as the man who gave it to me.'

'That's the master plan.' Erin's smile was wistful.

'About those rooms…' he said.

'Halfway along on your right,' said the girl. 'Checkout's at eleven and let me know if you need anything meantime.'

'Thanks.' And because she really was a sweet kid, even if she was far too young to be getting married, 'Nice ring.'

Tristan's room was functional and impersonal. He'd stayed in hundreds of rooms just like it over the years. A bed was a bed. A room was a room. It had never bothered him before. But it bothered him now. There was no warmth in it, no welcome. No… Erin.

Damn but he had it bad.

Jake would tell him to run, he knew that already, and Pete would ask him what he was waiting for. Luke would ask him searching questions he didn't want to answer—no way was he ringing Luke—and as for Hallie, there was no way he was calling her either. Hallie was crazy in love with her new husband and happier than he'd ever seen her…she'd be delighted that he'd finally let someone in.

As if he had a choice.

Erin knocked on Tristan's door as soon as she'd unpacked. It was only three-thirty and she wanted to visit some sapphire mines before the end of the day. She was anxious to find what she needed. Anxious to be on her way. She'd thought she could keep her distance from Tristan but, the more she knew of him, the harder it was. She'd thought she was resistant to such men. She'd thought he would keep *his* distance from *her*.

'I'm just going for a drive out to this place with the sale on,' she said when Tristan opened his door. 'You don't have to come, though. You'd probably rather stay here and catch up on some sleep.' They'd been up so early and he'd done most of the driving—nasty, rainy-day driving. He looked exhausted.

'I'll come,' he said.

'No, really. I'm just going to browse. You don't have to take your bodyguarding duties that seriously.'

'I'll come,' he said in a way that warned the discerning listener to beware the steel beneath. And that was the end of that.

Twenty minutes later they pulled into the car park of Wallace Sapphires, a medium-sized mining operation with its own onsite shop. There was a 'thirty per cent off marked price' sign on the shopfront door. Thirty per cent off everything.

The woman who looked up at them from behind the counter as they entered had a faded loveliness that matched her vintage clothing. Her eyes were shrewd but her smile was friendly as she greeted them with an invitation to look around and call her if there was anything they wanted to take a closer look at.

'I might get you to help me from the start,' said Erin, skirting a large tank of brilliantly coloured tropical fish that held centre stage in the shop. She pulled the opals from their Ziploc pouch and set them on the counter. 'I'm looking for sapphires the same colour as the blue in these opals. And I'm looking to buy in bulk.'

'May I?' The woman indicated a large magnifying glass set on a stand on the counter, and, at Erin's nod, set the opals beneath it. She peered down at the opals. 'They're quite beautiful, aren't they? Such a vivid blue.' And with a sigh, 'Most of our stones are darker. For this colour you really should be looking at Ceylon sapphires.'

'I know.' But she couldn't afford Ceylon sapphires. Not in the quantities she was after. 'I thought it was worth a try.'

'We did find colour like this once,' said the woman hesitantly. 'Came from a seam my late husband discovered more than twenty years ago. Good-sized stones they were too, but a terror to cut. We left most of them in the rough.'

'I don't mind buying rough stones.' Erin was sufficiently intrigued by the notion of gloriously coloured rough sapphires to want to see them. Even if they were hard to cut. 'Do you still have any?'

'You know, I think I might,' said the woman. 'Mind you, I have no idea where they are. Take a seat.' She gestured towards two stools on the customer side of the counter. 'This could take a while. My memory's not what it used to be. You wouldn't believe the things I've misplaced since Edward died. Gems, scissors, even the fish food… Why, if it wasn't for Roger I'm sure all the fish would be dead.'

'Who's Roger?' asked Tristan.

'A young work-experience boy we had here a few years back.' She was rifling through drawers as she spoke. 'He used to help us out in the school holidays when we were busy. Since Edward died he's been coming in every week to do the fish. He's due any minute and not a moment too soon. Those fish are starving. Ah, here they are. I'd filed them under "T". Probably for "Tragedy Waiting To Happen". Did I mention they were hard to cut?'

'Yes,' said Erin as the woman emptied the packet of stones onto the counter. 'But I'm feeling very optimistic about these stones.'

'What about the cutting of them?' asked Tristan.

'I'm optimistic about that too.' Rough sapphires were nothing like the finished stone. It took a discerning eye to predict the final colour of the stone and an even more discerning one to figure out how to cut it. She'd lose up to seventy-five per cent of the original weight of the stones in the cutting, but these stones were big. They'd still cut out at over half a carat and that was exactly what she wanted. Provided she could cut them.

The bell on the entry door tinkled and a young man in unironed clothes and a shabby baseball cap entered, carrying buckets, aquarium equipment, and a bag of multicoloured pebbles under one arm. This, decided Erin, was Roger.

'Afternoon, Mrs Wal,' he said, his cheerful nod encompassing them all as he headed for the fish tank. 'Afternoon, Lucinda.'

'Who's Lucinda?' asked Tristan.

'Lucinda's an angelfish,' said Roger, tapping the tank. 'This one here. Hello gorgeous.'

'Edward's pride and joy,' said the woman.

'Edward being Mrs Wal's deceased husband,' muttered Erin before Tristan could ask.

'I knew that,' he said.

'I got you some more fish food pellets,' said Roger, setting a small tin on top of the tank.

'Darling boy. How much do I owe you?'

'It's all right, Mrs Wal; it didn't cost much.'

'I wish you'd let me pay you,' she said, and Erin was in full agreement. Roger didn't look as if he had a lot to spare. 'How's the baby?'

'Fever's down and she's on the mend. She'll be right again in no time. I'll bring her out with me next week if you like,' he said as he set to work scooping pebbles from the tank. Mrs Wal's eyes brightened.

'She's such a dear little poppet,' she told them. 'You hardly know she's here.'

'You mentioned you'd misplaced some stones,' said Tristan as Erin positioned the magnifying glass over the sapphires and started sorting them with an eye to clarity, colour and shape. Her ears, however, were on the conversation.

'Seems to be happening a lot lately,' said Mrs Wal. 'I'll have them out and be showing them to customers one day and the next time I go looking for them I can't find them. I've been running this shop for thirty years. You'd think I'd know where to put everything by now.'

'Maybe you're not misplacing them,' said Tristan. 'Maybe someone's stealing from you. Low-level theft on a regular basis happens a lot.'

Erin looked sharply at Tristan. Tristan was looking at Mrs Wal. Mrs Wal was watching Roger clean the fish tank, and her eyes were sad.

'It's usually an employee,' said Tristan gently.

'It's possible,' she said as she dragged her gaze away from the fish tank to bestow on Tristan a wry and faded smile. 'But you know I think I'd rather believe I've misplaced them.'

Erin got an excellent deal on the sapphires. Two dozen rough stones of her choice and six smaller ones thrown in for free for cutting practice. 'I'll keep my fingers crossed for you,' said the older woman as she bagged the stones. 'If you can cut them you'll have some beautiful stones.'

'If I figure out the knack before I've used up all my practice stones I'll send those ones back to you, cut,' said Erin.

'You will not!' said Mrs Wal. 'Use them in your competition pieces and mind you let me know when you win.'

'*If* I win.'

'Is that one of your designs?' Mrs Wal gestured towards the tiger-eye pendant at Erin's throat.

Erin nodded.

'You'll win. The combination of those sapphires and those opals will be magnificent. You'll see.'

Erin did see. And lost herself in the vision.

'She's gone,' said Mrs Wal. 'I know that look.' Tristan smiled, and Mrs Wal blinked. 'My, you're a handsome one when you lose the sternness, aren't you? You should smile more often.'

'She's right,' Erin told him, coming back to the conversation with a sigh. 'You really do have the sweetest smile, but unlike Mrs Wal I'll not encourage it. Brood, be stern. You save those smiles.'

Tristan's smile widened.

Damn.

'You think Roger's stealing from Mrs Wal, don't you?' she said as they walked across the car park towards the car. Tristan's questions were rarely questions for the sake of small talk. He'd sensed something amiss back there in that shop. She knew he had.

'I think someone's stealing from her,' he said, shooting her a sideways glance. 'I don't necessarily know that it's Roger.'

'She could just be misplacing them, you know.'

'She didn't strike me as particularly forgetful. It took her all of two minutes to find those stones for you and I'm betting she hasn't had them out for years. No, she knows her stock and I suspect she knows she's not forgetting where she left it.'

'But that's terrible!' she said. 'Why doesn't she do something about it? *You* could do something. We could go back tomorrow and work through it with her.'

'What happened to forgetting about work for a while and chasing rainbows instead?'

'This is different.'

'No.' Tristan's smile was grim. 'It's just the same. There's a victim—in this case Mrs Wal—and there's a perp. Let's for argument's sake say that Roger is the perp. Roger's been helping out at Wallace Sapphires for years, possibly being paid for it, maybe not. He doesn't have much but he doesn't need it either. He makes do. And then one day he gets into a bind with money and the banks won't touch him and no one in his family's got it to give. He borrows a few thousand from the wrong kind of people and all of a sudden life takes a turn for the worse. He can't get work, his lenders want their money back, and he has a kid of his own and she's a sickly little thing, which means medicine and it ain't cheap. And there's Mrs Wallace with more sapphires than she can sell in a lifetime and surely she won't miss one little stone… So he takes one. And then another,' said Tristan savagely. 'Before he knows it he's thieving regularly and vowing that one day, *one* day, he'll give it all back. Meanwhile he'll give it back in help and somehow try to convince himself that he's not really hurting anyone, that it's not such a crime as far as crimes go, and that it's the only way he can survive. Who's the victim, Erin?' said Tristan bleakly. 'And how the hell are you going to go back in there tomorrow and fix it?'

She'd wanted this, she remembered belatedly. She'd wanted Tristan to open up and talk about his work. Well, now he had.

'It might not be like that,' she said in a small voice.

'No,' he said. 'It might not.' But it was clear that his faith in the justice system he'd sworn to uphold was badly damaged.

'This is what happens when you go undercover, isn't it? You get too close, too involved.'

Tristan was silent, his features grim.

'And then you have to turn around and make impossible decisions about impossible situations and it doesn't always make things right, does it? Sometimes all it does is make things worse.'

Nothing.

'It can't always be like that,' she said a touch desperately. 'Sometimes you make things better.'

'Yeah,' he said with a weary smile that pierced her to the core. 'Sometimes we do.'

It wasn't supposed to be like this, thought Erin grimly. She wasn't supposed to stare at him in dismayed silence because his problem was too big and there was no fixing it. She should have been able to comfort him. With wise words and compassion or whatever it was that he needed. She should have been able to help.

A bad call. Maybe even the right call but the wrong result. *This* was what Tristan dealt with on a daily basis. This was why the nightmares and the disillusion, and she had no answers other than for him to step back and not care so much and let someone else enforce society's rules, at least for a little while.

She wanted to help him. Needed to think that she could. She simply didn't know how.

They got in the car in silence. Tristan the driver and she in the passenger seat. It was her turn to drive but she didn't push the issue. He'd broken his silence and would see it as weakness. And curse himself for letting her see it.

His features were stern and forbidding as he started the car and pulled out of the car park. The rain had stopped but there would be no sunset this night. No hot pools or mud fights to ease the tension. She wanted it gone. Contrary woman that she was she desperately wanted to win a smile from him. But how? She stared out the window at the passing landscape, thinking.

They were in granite country, sheep country for the

most part, and that meant rolling grassland punctuated by the occasional stockyard and shearing shed. No inspiration there, she thought glumly. Unless… 'Hey, there's an old bomb just like the one you bought off Frank.'

'Where?' Tristan slowed the car.

'Over by the shearing shed. To the left. Half buried in grass.' Now that she looked more closely it didn't really resemble the car he'd bought from Frank at all.

'It's an FJ Holden ute,' said Tristan. From the tone of his voice, this was a good thing.

'We've stopped.'

'We have to take a closer look at it.'

She got out of the car willingly enough and followed Tristan towards it. There was something in his eyes when he looked at that old wreck that she wouldn't destroy for the world. It was hope.

'Look at the lines on her,' he said when they were standing beside it.

The lines that remained were lovely. The rest were the product of an impressive imagination.

'I could restore it,' he said. 'I wonder if it runs?'

Erin was wondering if it had an engine at all.

It didn't.

'I could put a BBQ under the bonnet,' he said, in no way deterred. 'Or a pizza oven.'

'You could turn it into a garden ornament,' she said. 'A water feature with water sheeting down the windscreen and the wipers wiping it off. The neighbours would love it.'

'I could use it for storage,' he said, sticking his head inside the body of the car. 'Like Frank was using the Ford.'

'You'd need doors, of course,' she said. 'But the lack of seats would be a definite advantage.'

'I could turn it into a dog kennel.'

'I didn't know you had a dog.'

He walked around the old truck a few times and finally stood back to admire it from afar. 'I think I'll make an offer on it,' he said.

Erin nodded, flashed him a grin. 'I think you should.'

'Dinner,' said Erin, 'should be about celebration.'

'You mean balloons?' said Tristan. He'd tried to retreat, tried to pull back when they'd returned to the motel, but Erin was blocking him every step of the way.

'I mean good food, good wine, a pleasant atmosphere and lively company. But I'll take three out of four.'

'You don't think the food will be any good?'

'Ooh, a joke. I'm *very* impressed. I'm thinking we should eat at the pub. Best char-grilled steaks and pleasant atmosphere in town. It says so right here on the flyer.'

'It's called promotion,' he said dryly.

'And it's very effective,' she said. 'Because my mouth is watering as we speak. What do you say?'

She was in his room again, perched on the edge of the table and wielding sunshine like a sword. 'I'm really tired,' was what he said.

'And so you should be. Which is why we're heading down there now rather than later. Imagine how well you'll sleep on a stomach full of steak and potatoes.'

He did like steak and potatoes. 'Do I need to get changed?'

'No, perfection is fine.' She eyed his jeans and T-shirt and sighed. 'How do I look?'

'Fine.' She was wearing a sky-blue sundress, strappy little sandals, and half a dozen thin gold bracelets at her wrist. She was beautiful.

'You know how you were saying you liked to keep the sweet talk for later? I'm guessing you like to save the compliments for later too.'

'You want a compliment?'

She nodded firmly. 'And sweet talk too.'

'I like your shoes,' he said.

'I'm taking that as the sweet talk. Now for the compliment.'

Tristan stifled a smile. 'May I think about it over dinner?'

Her eyes narrowed. 'Certainly. But I have to warn you, I'm not a patient woman.'

'I noticed that,' he said amiably. 'Good thing you're so beautiful.'

'That wasn't a compliment.'

'No,' he said. 'I'm still working on that.'

'Good thing *you're* so beautiful,' she muttered. 'Shall we go?'

The Brasserie at the pub was all dark carpet, wooden panelling, and comfortably mismatched furniture. The lighting was friendly rather than intimate and the bustle from the bar and the thoroughfare to the poker machines and gaming area gave it a relaxing informality. It was just what Tristan needed, Erin decided.

Sometimes it was nice to sit back and watch the world go by.

'I'm for the rib fillet and salad,' she said after examining the blackboard menu. Tristan chose rump and three veg. 'Shall we argue about who's paying for this now or later?' she said.

Tristan shrugged. 'I'm easy.'

That he wasn't.

'We can argue about it whenever you like.'

She chose now. 'I'd like to thank you for coming on this trip with me,' she said earnestly. 'For your time and effort. I would like to buy you a meal. *This* meal. And the drinks.'

Tristan regarded her steadily. 'You never give up, do you?'

'You're wrong,' she said. 'I'm fairly focussed on what I want to achieve, yes, but the truth is my resolve has never really been tested. I've never, for example, been in a burning building and had to pull out even though I knew there were still people inside. Rory was the one who had to do that.'

'Nothing else he could have done,' said Tristan.

'Try telling him that.' She wasn't finished yet. 'Nor have I ever lost two men in a mine clearing operation and the following day sent another team in to replace them. My father has. I think I'd have given up and gone home.'

'Your father's been trained to make tough decisions.'

'He has, and he does. It's the living with them afterwards that's the problem. My father's a good man. A strong man. So's Rory. I'm proud of them both. But sometimes they hurt in places that I can't reach, and I can't help them and it drives me nuts.' She took a deep breath and said it plain. 'I look at you and you're just the same. Hurting in places I can't reach. And it drives me nuts.'

'You help,' he said quietly. 'By being there. By being you.'

God! If they didn't change the topic soon she was going to cry. 'Was that your compliment?'

'No. Still working on that.'

'Work faster—I'm feeling a little fragile.' There was a folded newspaper on the chair beside her. She picked it up, opened it out. Horoscopes. Tristan, if she remembered correctly, was a Scorpio. 'It says here that you'll be receiving a boon, and that power mixed with love will give you grace.'

'Humph.'

'You're right,' she said. 'You've already got the grace thing covered.'

She moved on to the Virgo section. 'It says here that *my* power this week lies not in understanding but in giving. It says that rich rewards will come to Virgos who learn this lesson. Well, I guess that settles it.'

'Settles what?' he asked warily.

'I am definitely paying for this meal.'

The food was good, the wine was excellent, and the atmosphere was indeed very pleasant. Erin was halfway through her meal when she saw Roger the fish-tank cleaner walking into the room carrying a little blonde poppet who couldn't have been more than a year old. He nodded to the barman, who angled his head towards the poker-machine room. Roger said something to the tot, who nodded and gave him a watery smile and then the pair of them disappeared into the gaming room. 'Was that Roger?' she said to Tristan.

Tristan nodded.

Five minutes later, Roger reappeared. He still had the little girl cradled in one arm, but walking beside him, holding his other hand, was a young woman with big sad eyes and a pinched face. She looked defiant. Dejected. Roger looked resigned. They were halfway across the room when Roger spotted them. Recognition crossed his face before he quickly looked away.

She thought that was it, that he wouldn't look back, but then Roger's eyes sought Tristan's again and something passed between them. A question maybe, or an answer. She didn't know.

It seemed an age before Roger's gaze cut to her. He gave her what might have once passed for a smile if not for the misery in it, and then he and his little entourage moved on.

'You *do* think it was Roger who took those sapphires, don't you?'

'Yes,' said Tristan.

'What would the police do if they caught him?'

'Arrest him. Send him to court.'

'What would the court do?'

'Send him to prison.'

'What would *you* do?'

'I just did it.'

'Leaned on him? Is that what that look between you was about?'

'No,' he said, his lips tilting ever so slightly. 'You'd know it if I decided to lean on someone.'

'Well, what was it about?'

'Recognition. It was about knowing what he was. Maybe even knowing why he was doing it. And letting it go. Mrs Wal herself doesn't want to follow through on this one, Erin. And neither do I.'

She stared at him solemnly. Saw the strength there and the compassion. And without any thought for an audience of strangers she put her hand to his cheek and kissed him softly on the lips. Not passion, not this time. This was something else.

'What was that for?' His sudden stillness was disconcerting; those glorious amber eyes of his were intent.

'For doing what you do,' she said. 'For being the man you are.' And because she was in love with him.

Erin paid for their meal. Paid for their drinks and Tristan let her. It was written in the stars, she'd told him loftily. Besides, she'd said next, it was either that or a tiger-eye signet ring.

She twisted him with words, spun him into knots. And with laughter on her lips and wisdom in her eyes, spun him round again.

Work talk, when he never talked about his work with anyone.

Encouraging him to buy another old car wreck. What the hell was he going to do with two of them? He didn't even know what he was going to do with one.

Rock climbing! Enough said.

'What time do you want to get up in the morning?' she asked him as they headed for the car.

'No more sapphires?' he asked gruffly. She'd kissed him gently in the pub and stopped his heart.

'No,' she said solemnly. 'I have everything I need now as far as making jewellery is concerned. We can go home. We could have an early night, get up in the morning, and drive back to Sydney.'

She'd looked at him with pride and something else and he'd damn near wept.

He made it to the car, to the door of his motel room before he stopped her. He thought it showed a remarkable degree of restraint. 'I have nothing to give you,' he muttered. 'I'm not what you want.' And still he reached for her.

'I know,' she said. And still she came.

Tender, he could be that, at least for a little while as he pressed his lips to hers. Slow and easy as he gave her every chance to pull back while she still could. While he could still let her. 'I don't know where I'll be in a month's time or what I'll be doing. I don't want to hurt you.'

'I'm glad to hear it.' She punctuated her words with a nip to his bottom lip and desire ripped through him, fierce and needy. He wanted to be in control. Needed to think that he could be. His words were meant to keep her at bay. To keep them both safe, and she was playing the game, heaven help him she was. He found the frantic pulse at the base of her neck with his lips and nipped with his teeth, darkly pleased when she gasped and arched into him. Maybe he did want to hurt her, just a little bit. Maybe he wanted her burning up for him the way he burned for her. Filling him, dammit, with everything that she was.

Her eyes were dark and fey as she pulled his head back to stare up at him. 'I won't ask you for tomorrow,

Tristan. Nothing you don't want. But I will ask something of you tonight.'

'What is it?'

'When we're making love… When I'm wrapped around you and I can't feel anything but you inside of me, can't see anyone but you above me…don't you dare try to control it. Don't you dare hold back.'

'God!' he muttered.

He managed to get the door open, managed to get her inside before he pushed her back against the wall and savaged her mouth. He was undone, he couldn't think. There was nothing but Erin and his need to have her and it was overwhelming. The room was in darkness once he'd slammed the door shut but he didn't reach for the light switch. He wanted it dark as he hiked up her dress with greedy hands and ripped the thin, lacy barrier of her panties aside. Her hands were at his T-shirt, pushing it up his chest, and then it was off, and her lips were at the base of his neck and moving lower. He freed himself, lifted her against the wall and her legs came around him and he cursed her, cursed himself, and then the gods for good measure as he slammed into her where they stood.

She cried out when he entered her, not in shock but in sheer outrageous pleasure. She was ready for him, had always been ready for him, and she wrapped her arms around his neck as sensation piled in on her and she surrendered to wherever he wanted to take her. Wherever he wanted to go.

Harder, he drove her there and she met him thrust for vicious thrust. Deeper, she took him there, darkly delighted when he cursed again, even as his hands curved around her thighs and he positioned her for still more. He was greedy and desperate and he was all that mattered. All she'd ever wanted.

She thrust her hands in his hair, she wanted to see his face, and caught her breath when she did because he wasn't in control. She was his and he was lost. Mindlessly, magnificently lost. And then his mouth was on hers again, hot and wild as he took her higher and higher still, took her to the very edge of pleasure. And tipped her over.

She was like quicksilver. Gloriously, unashamedly wanton as she came apart in his arms and there was nothing for it but to follow her. Nothing he could do but pour himself into her, over and over, as he found his own pulsing release. He felt her go limp in his arms. Felt himself tremble as he slapped his hand against the wall for balance. She was breathing hard and shuddering in the aftermath. So was he. 'God, I hope that was what you had in mind,' he muttered.

Her smile was shaky, but it was there. 'It was perfect.'

'Good.' Because he wanted more.

CHAPTER EIGHT

THEY made it to the bed this time and Tristan was careful with Erin as he tugged the cover aside and lowered her onto the sheets. 'I don't know whether to get you out of that dress or not.' He came down on the bed beside her, leaning on one elbow to look at her. 'You look so incredibly wanton in it.' It would have to come off, of course, but for now…for now he thought he might be able to move a little slower if she left it on.

He needed to touch her this time and to linger. He needed to show her that he could be careful with a woman. That he knew tenderness as well as insatiable need. He wanted light this time too, and the dim glow of the bedside lamp was just enough. He needed to see her eyes.

'I could keep it on a while longer, I guess.' Her eyes were dark and full of lazy satisfaction. 'But sooner or later it's going to come off. You know that, don't you?'

He knew.

'I want your skin against mine. All of it.'

'You'll have it,' he muttered, for he could deny her nothing. 'Later.' He slid his hand beneath her dress and trailed it up her body, and everywhere he touched he drew a response. A gasp, a shudder, a plea. And then he slowly brought his hand down to where she was hot and wet and open for him.

He knew how to pleasure a woman, thought Erin hazily as he found her with his fingers. Knew exactly how to please her as his lips found the curve of her jaw and his fingers worked their magic. Too much, too soon, and there was nothing she could do about it. She was his. Utterly and irrevocably his, to do with what he wished, and if that meant he wanted her to come for him again with nothing but the stroke of his fingers and a layer of clothing between them then she would. Again and again and again.

That didn't mean she couldn't try and change his focus somewhat.

She put her hand over his and arched into both, and then she was trailing her fingers up his arm, revelling in the contrast of silky skin over hard, hard muscle. His was a warrior's body, tough and lean, and she couldn't get enough of it. Couldn't resist tracing the sculpted contours of his chest, and all the time he was playing her with *his* hands. Playing her to perfection.

She felt the heat rising through her, felt her breath quicken, and resisted. Not yet, not like this. She wanted…more. She slid her hand to his shoulders, to the nape of his neck, and then she was drawing him towards her. She wanted his lips on hers, and then they were and it was so much more than she'd ever dreamed of. He was all darkness and heat and his mouth took her so deep, so fast, that she came apart in his arms for the second time that night. And cursed him in the aftermath.

'What was that for?' He was half indignant and wholly amused. 'Shouldn't you be thanking me?'

'Thank you,' she said grudgingly. '*Now* can I take my dress off?'

'No. I'm *trying* to show you a little consideration here. Slow things down. You're not cooperating.'

She started to laugh. 'Kiss me less. Touch me less. That might help.'

'Not sure that's possible. I'm thinking of kissing you more. Stand up.'

'I *know* that's not possible.' But she did it anyway and stood there before him in a crumpled blue dress with an ache for this deep, brooding man that she knew now would never fade. He came to her then, circled her like a hawk, with an eye to weakness, but the only weakness was her heart and that was in strong hands already. His hands. She lifted her chin high as he looked his fill and then he was behind her, his fingers barely brushing her skin as he found the zipper of her dress and slowly drew it down. He smoothed the straps from her shoulders next and then the dress was gone, pooled in a puddle at her feet and she was naked. 'Finally.'

'You know, maybe you shouldn't talk at all,' he said. 'Comments like that could make a man want to rush things.' He punctuated his words with a feather-light kiss to the sensitive curve of her neck. Maybe he had a point. He could be gentle when he wanted to be, she thought, and trembled when he ran his fingertips slowly down her spine and over her behind. And then he was in front of her, shucking off his trousers and then they were both naked and he was drawing her closer, skin on skin, and his mouth came down on hers, dreamy and magical as he took the time to savour her.

She gave too much, he thought, when he thought at all. So warm, so smooth in his arms as he took the time, this time, to learn what she liked. His lips at her collarbone made her tremble. Trailing a finger across her breast and over her tight little nipple made her gasp. She copied his movements exactly, tracing her fingers over his nipple and letting them linger and *he* gasped. And then, with a wicked little smile, she took his nipple in her mouth and he almost lost his mind. Again.

So generous, too generous, and her laughter was dark and damning as he tumbled her onto the bed, coming down over her, all thought of tenderness forgotten as passion roared through him. He couldn't get enough of her, the taste of her skin, the scent of her, her slightness and her strength. She was fearless, and fascinating, and, heaven help them both, she held nothing back, offering him whatever he wanted, and he wanted it all.

He took her breast with his mouth and she screamed her approval. Set his lips to her waist and she jackknifed in his arms as if she'd been shot.

'Hurry,' she said, but he was already there, pinning her to the bed and dragging her hands above her head even as her legs came around him and he buried himself inside her. 'Tristan, please…' Her eyes were wild with need, her body taut with it. 'I can't wait—'

'Yes, you can,' he commanded. 'Look at me.' He brushed her lips with his. 'Feel me.' He kissed her again and felt his control slip away. 'Come with me,' he whispered, and, locking eyes with her, he began to move.

* * *

Tristan dreamt of the dockyards of Prague and a night that was rife with despair. A thick mist eddied around his feet and the air was sharp with salt and the unmistakable scent of death. Anguish rolled over him like a wave, spinning him round, working him over, and he turned away abruptly. He'd waited too long.

'No.' Shudders racked his body, even as he clenched his fists and willed himself to stop. To make his face impassive as he watched the team from the coroner's office bag the last of the bodies. He was a cop. He *knew* the depths humanity could sink to. But he'd never seen the likes of this.

The drone of a ship horn melded with another sound, an inarticulate cry of anger and grief. The sound was close; it might have come from him; he didn't know.

'Shh.' There was another voice in this nightmare, a different voice, and it was Erin, smoothing his hair from his face with gentle fingers as she leaned over him. 'It's all right. It's just a dream.'

'No.' He was still caught in sleep but it wasn't a dream. That much he did know.

'It's all right,' she murmured, and put her palm to his heart as if to stem the frantic beating of it.

He reached for her, gathered her close and drew a deep and ragged breath, breathing her in, the warm, feminine scent of her that chased away the memory of a raw and fetid stench. 'Erin, they're dead,' he said hoarsely. 'They're all dead. I was too late.'

'Shh.' Her arms came around him tightly, protectively. 'It's all right now. It's over.' He felt her lips in his hair as she cradled him into her body and it was shelter from the darkness and the home he'd never found. 'I've got you,' she whispered.

With a shuddering sigh, Tristan slept.

CHAPTER NINE

TRISTAN woke with the dawn the following morning, took one look at the sleeping woman curled into his side with her head on his shoulder and a hand on his heart, and felt a fear so big and overwhelming that he simply had to escape. He dressed fast and silently and hightailed it out of that room as if a horde of demons were after him. She gave too much. And he who'd spent a lifetime never taking too much had taken it all.

He'd dreamed last night; at least he thought he had. The same nightmare, only this time he hadn't woken in a sweat. He'd slipped out of it somehow and that was Erin's doing; he knew it instinctively, even if he couldn't remember how it had happened.

Not love. He repeated it to himself fiercely as he took to the sidewalk and headed towards the town centre. Never that. As he replayed last night's events over and over in his mind.

And knew himself for a liar.

When Erin woke the following morning she was in Tristan's motel room in Tristan's bed. Alone. She rolled onto her back and stared up at the dreary grey ceiling, not sure if she was grateful for the solitude or hurt by it. Making love with Tristan had been more than she'd ever dreamed of. Wilder, faster, more intense than anything she'd ever known. More…everything. She stretched experimentally and felt her body protest. Her body ached because of him, and damned if it didn't still ache *for* him, even after last night.

Especially after last night.

Clothes. She found her dress by the bed, her shoes and panties over by the door. Right where she'd left them. There was no sign of Tristan's clothes, although his carryall was still there. No sign of Tristan either. She needed a shower. Didn't know whether to take one in his room or head next door to hers. A door between them would have been useful. An adjoining door.

Her room would be better. Fresh clothes were there. Her toiletries. And when Tristan returned to his room she would not be there; she thought that bit was important. She was standing in the middle of the room, naked, just about to get dressed when she heard the sound of a key in the door. Moments later she was face to face with Tristan and feeling incredibly self-conscious, which was ridiculous given the liberties he'd taken with her body last night.

'You're back,' she said awkwardly.

'I, er…yes.' He came in, shut the door carefully behind him and set the bakery bag on the table.

'I was just—'

'I just went out for—'

They spoke in unison. Stopped in unison.

He tried again. 'I didn't mean to…' he gestured

towards her nakedness, trying hard to stay unaffected '…ah, interrupt whatever…'

'The shower,' she said hurriedly.

'In there.' He was pretty sure that was where it was.

'Yes,' she said. 'Yes, it is. I'll, er, go, then.' And with a glance that was half mortified and half amused, she fled into the bathroom.

The minute she shut the door Tristan cursed and ran a hand through his hair. He wasn't a boy. He was thirty years old. He was no stranger to waking up with a woman in his bed. Nothing permanent, but he was civilised enough to offer them the use of his shower and have coffee made by the time they reappeared. Backing off easy, keeping it casual.

Jake had once asked him how the hell he got away with it and his reply had been simple. You laid down the ground rules beforehand. Jake had snorted and shook his head. And asked him how he ever got a woman to agree to *them*.

He *had* laid down the ground rules last night, hadn't he? He was pretty sure he had. Right there, just outside the door. Just before he'd gone insane. So now all he had to do was re-establish them and figure out a strategy for keeping his distance for the rest of the day.

Concentration was important. He planned to drive a lot. Keep his mind on the road and off the woman who sat beside him. She was good at sneaking past his defences. She was the daughter of a military man. She knew the value of strategy and the element of surprise. Of laughter and misdirection. She was smart.

Sneaky.

She was ten minutes in the shower.

Ten very long minutes during which time he tried very hard to forget what they'd shared during the night. He made the bed. That helped. Packed his duffel and sat it by the door. Also a good move. Coffee came next and he set about boiling the jug, ripping coffee and sugar sachets open and dumping them into mugs. He'd almost managed to get his thoughts back in order when she emerged from the shower and scattered them again as he tried to remember what it was he was supposed to be doing. Keeping his distance. Well, he was, wasn't he? He hadn't reached for her at all yet. He was doing just fine. As well as could be expected.

After a night like that.

She looked beautiful in her crumpled blue dress. Rested. How on earth she pulled *that* off he didn't know, because she certainly hadn't had much sleep. She smiled at him and her smile was warm and easy, which was both good and bad. Her awkwardness seemed to have disappeared. His, on the other hand, seemed to be growing. 'Juice?' he offered.

'From the bar fridge?'

'From the bakery. Breakfast roll?'

She looked at the bakery bag on the counter, looked at him. 'You're feeding me?'

Damn. He knew walking into that bakery had been a mistake. 'Don't dwell on it.'

She smiled and reached for the bag of bread rolls and the tension in his stomach eased. 'I've been thinking,' she said, and the ache in his stomach was back, only this time it was multiplied tenfold. He hated it when a woman got to thinking. Especially the morning after. 'You didn't give me a compliment last night at dinner.'

'I didn't?' He narrowed his eyes. 'You're very smart.'

'Backhanded compliments don't count,' she said, shaking her head. 'I want a genuine one.'

'Working on it.'

Her smile was pure challenge. 'I'm glad to hear it. Is that coffee?'

'I wasn't sure how you took it.' He had all the fixings there. He just hadn't made it.

'White, no sugar.'

Girl coffee. He made it fast and set it on the table beside her, deliberately not handing it to her directly, because handing it to her meant touching her and touching her was out.

'So…' she said, after she'd sipped her coffee and nibbled on her bun, 'I'm thinking we need lots of inane morning-after conversation.'

'Silence is good,' he countered. 'Silence is golden.'

'No.' She eyed him steadily. 'We do not want golden this morning. We want casual and meaningless. At least, I'm assuming that's what you want.'

It was. He was desperate for it. Whether they could manage it was a different matter altogether. 'Nice day outside,' he said doggedly. 'Rain's gone.'

'That's good.' She smiled at him and sipped her coffee. 'Did you know that Inverell has an old-car museum?'

'That's not inane,' he said indignantly. 'That's important.'

'Hmm. It opens to the public at nine a.m. When did you want to leave for Sydney?'

'When do *you* want to leave?'

'It's an eight-hour drive, straight down the New England,' she said matter-of-factly. 'We could leave at lunchtime and still get home this evening. If you wanted to.'

'Or if you wanted to,' he said.

'Mmm.' She handed him a glass of orange juice. 'Cheers.'

She was doing it deliberately. Holding off until *he* said something about where they were going and when. As if *he* knew.

'Had any more thoughts about that compliment?'

'No.' He wasn't currently thinking complimentary thoughts about her at all and one look at the smirk she was trying to hide behind her orange juice told him she knew it. Damned if she didn't think she had the upper hand in not-nearly-as-inane-as-it-seemed conversation this morning. The fact that she *did* didn't improve his mood any.

It was half eight already. It would take half an hour to eat, shower, and get underway. After that it was straight down the road. He *did* want to get back to Sydney today. Didn't he?

'Here's the plan,' he said. 'First the car museum, then a quick stop at Wallace Sapphires. After that we hit the highway and head for home.'

'Why Wallace Sapphires?'

Tristan rubbed the back of his neck. For all that this wasn't his beat or his business he couldn't let Roger keep stealing from the widow Wallace. 'I thought I might speak with Mrs Wallace about protecting her sapphires from theft. Simple measures like a security camera in the shop, for instance.'

'Or finding another fish-tank cleaner.'

'That too. The point is, she has options. She should know that.'

'I like it.'

Erin's smile warmed him through. Spun him round. He didn't want it. Didn't need it. He told himself that as he stood there watching her and wondering just what it was about her that made her so different from any other woman he'd ever known. 'I need a shower,' he muttered.

'And I'm off to pack.' She downed her coffee, collected her shoes, and started to leave. Her steps slowed as she drew level with him and her smile faltered as her eyes searched his face. 'If I thought I could pull it off I'd kiss you good morning,' she said solemnly. 'One of those quick, thanks-for-the-good-time-last-night kisses. One that said I was used to feeling the way I felt when I was in your arms. That's the kind of kiss I'd give you this morning. If I thought I could pull it off.'

'Erin?' She was halfway out the door before he spoke. 'If I thought I could pull it off I'd let you.'

Erin didn't mind taking a wander through the old-car museum. There were other things there to look at besides cars. Old petrol-station pumps and shopfront signs. Porcelain dolls.

Tristan…

She really, really liked seeing the boyish side of Tristan come out to play. She'd tease it out more often if he were hers. Make sure it appeared at least once daily to counteract the seriousness of his work.

No! She had to stop thinking about what she would do if he were hers. He wasn't hers. He didn't want to be hers. And that was a good thing because he was everything she didn't want in a partner. Work he couldn't talk about. Hurt she couldn't heal. And a dedication to duty that he simply couldn't shake.

Oh, he was trying, she thought with grim humour. He was hurt enough, and tired enough to wonder about finding another job. A more menial job. And two months into that he'd wonder what on earth he was doing there. His need to make a difference, to make the world or at least the part of it he walked through a better place, was too strong.

So they would call in to Wallace Sapphires on the way home today and he would do what he did. With compassion and with grace he would serve and protect.

It was ten-thirty before they left the museum. He'd immersed himself in yesteryear and lingered longer than he should have, thought Tristan, but the old jalopies, some perfectly restored and some not, had been impossible to resist. Erin could have hurried him along but she hadn't. She'd given him space and walked her own path through the museum, an easy wander that had taken in the little curiosities more so than the cars, but if her aim was to put some distance between them, both literally and figuratively, she hadn't succeeded. Even surrounded by a hundred classic cars he always knew where she was. He knew when she was watching him, and he knew when she looked away. It was then that he looked at her. She was in his head. And he couldn't get her out.

It was almost eleven before they pulled into the Wallace Sapphire mine car park. 'What are you going to do if Mrs Wal isn't in the shop today?' asked Erin as he opened the car door.

'Find her. Wait in the car.'

'I'm coming with you.'

'No.'

'Clearly one of your favourite words,' she muttered as she got out of the car and met his gaze over the roof of it. 'It's like this. You can try and tie me to the car— and under different circumstances I might enjoy letting you—or I can come with you. I won't interfere—'

'Then stay in the car!'

'But I won't be left out. This isn't some official investigation, Tristan. You know it isn't. It's you and me trying to help an old lady with an employee problem.'

His glare was his blackest and he knew for a fact that it could reduce grown men to stuttering, but not Erin. Hands on her hips, she traded him glare for glare before dismissing him and heading for the shop.

He was one step behind her when she reached the door. One step ahead of her as he reached for the door handle and turned it for her. 'One of these days I really will shackle you to the car,' he muttered.

'Bite me.'

'That would come after,' he said, and meant every word of it.

Erin's eyes grew dark and slumberous. The grin she gave him was lethal. 'Promise?'

'Keep your mind on the job,' he muttered. 'That way maybe I can keep my mind on it too.'

'I'm on it,' she said, and with a deep breath, 'sorry.'

'First rule of policing.' She looked so contrite that he couldn't resist bringing his hand up to tuck a wayward strand of silky brown hair behind her ear. 'Never hit on your partner.'

'Right.' She took the hand he'd used to touch her with and brushed her lips against his knuckles, sending a jolt of desire straight through him.

'Why are we doing this *now*?' he muttered.

'Because right now we're safe. We know we have to stop,' she said with a tiny tilt of her lips as she let go of his hand and drew away.

Her words made a frightening amount of sense.

'Looks like we're in luck,' she said, peering through the door. 'There's Mrs Wal.'

'She's probably wondering why we're making out on her doorstep,' he muttered as he pushed the door open and ushered Erin into the shop. 'If she asks, *you* explain it.'

'If she asks, I will. Morning, Mrs Wal,' she said cheerfully.

'Oh, dear,' said the older woman with a tentative smile that didn't quite reach her eyes. 'It's going to be one of those days, I can tell. You've changed your mind about the sapphires, haven't you?'

'Not at all,' said Erin. 'Those sapphires are perfect.'

The widow Wallace looked relieved. 'Well, if there's anything else I can help you with…'

'Actually, we haven't come to look around,' Tristan said gently. 'I'm in law enforcement, Mrs Wallace, and

I'd like to talk to you about some options you might like to think about with regards to those missing sapphires. Nothing official,' he said at the older woman's look of alarm. 'But if they're being stolen rather than misplaced there are things you can do to protect your stock.'

Her eyes watered and she gave him a tremulous smile. 'You've a good heart,' she said. 'I knew it the first time I saw you. And I thank you for your concern, but it's not necessary.' She looked down at a closely written sheet of paper beside her on the counter.

'I found this tucked underneath the front door when I came in this morning. It lists every stone he ever took from me along with dates, prices, and calculated interest.' She looked as if she was about to cry. He hated it when they cried. He looked to Erin. Maybe she could help when it came to the tears. Nope. She looked as if *she* was going to cry. This was a disaster.

'This next sheet's a repayment schedule,' said the widow Wallace, picking it up and handing it to him. 'Starting today, of how he's going to pay it back.'

'Roger?' he asked gently and she nodded.

'These,' she said in a slightly firmer voice for which Tristan was truly thankful, 'are *my* calculations, using the cost price of the stones instead of retail price. I've used a lower interest rate as well. I knew he was in trouble, not that he ever said. That wife of his…' She shook her head. 'I'm offering him a job. I should have had someone in to oversee the business well before now. Lord knows my heart's not in it, not since Edward passed on. Besides, it's about time someone offered that boy a chance.'

'You'll be running a risk,' he said as he set the sheet on the counter beside her. It was a solution, yes. But it wasn't one he would have advised.

'I know.'

'What if he steals from you again?'

Mrs Wallace looked down at Roger's letter, at his estimate of what he'd taken and what he owed her, and smiled through her tears. 'He's a good boy,' she said. 'I know he is. Sometimes you've just got to have faith.'

'That went well,' said Erin when they reached the car. 'Not quite what I expected, mind, but it certainly *feels* like a win for the good guys. I feel good about this. Mrs Wal feels good about this.' She stared at Tristan's stern profile. He was doing the driving again. 'Do *you* feel good about this?'

'I'm not unhappy about it,' he said after a while. 'I believe in giving people a second chance.'

'I'm hearing a but,' she said.

'But I'm not a big believer in happily ever afters either,' he said quietly. 'I don't see it.'

'What about hope?' she asked him. 'Do you see that?'

'Yeah,' he said. 'Lately I do.'

They stopped for a late lunch in Tamworth and even after they'd lingered over coffee they were making good time. Erin took a stint at the wheel and then it was his turn again, as the sun slipped behind the horizon and the night unfolded. They would get home that evening, without a doubt, thought Tristan. They would get home and say goodbye and he would walk away unscathed and so would she. That was what he wanted. What they both wanted. Wasn't it?

She didn't like what he did for a living.

Yet she understood it instinctively. She knew the heaviness that came with duty and by God she knew how to fight it. With laughter and hope and a hefty dose of distraction, she brought balance into a world that was too often too dark.

He lived in London.

But he wouldn't be going back there. Not to live. He wanted a transfer back to Australia and a break from undercover work. He could make it happen.

He was scared witless of giving his heart to a woman and then losing her.

There was that.

No woman had ever captivated him so completely, or made him fear so much. He didn't know how she did it, she just did and she was everything he'd ever needed and everything he'd never allowed himself to dream of.

'Whoa!' she said suddenly.

'What?' he said, alarmed. 'What is it?'

'Kangaroo,' she said. 'A big grey one. Huge. It was just about to hop out in front of us.'

'I didn't see it.'

'Could have been a wombat, I guess.'

'A *wombat*?'

'Big grey one.'

He saw the tilt of her lips out of the corner of his eye. He was too busy looking for kangaroos and oversized wombats to look at her properly.

There was nothing there.

'Dangerous business, this driving down the highway at dusk,' she said conversationally.

'Yeah.' Particularly with a madwoman in the car.

'There's a motel a few kilometres up ahead. We passed a sign a couple of kilometres back.'

'Was that before or after you saw the mutant kanga-rombat?'

'I'm pretty sure it was just before.'

He chanced a glance at her. Her smile was wicked.

'Maybe we should consider spending the night at the motel,' she said. 'For the sake of the animals. I'm all for protecting rare and endangered wildlife.'

He had to smile. Even as he cursed her and surrendered to the inevitable. He didn't want to make it home tonight. He didn't want the trip to end, didn't want to have to say goodbye to her. Not…yet. 'You're right,' he said. 'We should do our bit for wildlife conservation.'

'I do like conviction in a man.' She stretched languidly and sent him a smile that slid through him like a hot knife through butter. 'How many rooms do you think we'll be needing?'

'One.'

They made it to the room without touching. He managed to get their bags in and the door closed before he reached for her. 'Kiss me good morning,' he muttered as her arms came around his neck, and her eyes grew dreamy.

'I looked for you this morning, when I woke,' she whispered as she brushed her lips across his. 'I wanted your lips on mine. I wanted mine on you.' She set her mouth to his and her kiss was deep, and drugging, and seemed to last for ever. 'I watched you at the car museum and I wanted to kiss you then. Right there by the straight-eight Ford you fell in love with.' Her fingers were at his shirt, unbuttoning it and smoothing it over his shoulders and he let her, helplessly following the flow of emotion that bound him to her. 'I watched your gentleness with Mrs Wallace and wanted it for myself. I still want it.' And then her lips were on his again and he was slowly drowning in her. He felt the edge of passion rip through him and fought to control it. Not yet. Mindless desire didn't always rule him. He could be gentle, *would* be gentle. Because this time he needed to give as well as take.

So he slowed his hands as he slid them over her, slowed his movements as he drew her down onto the bed and took the time to savour what he held.

She sighed, shakily as he undressed her, his hands gentle and sure. There was passion in him, there always was, but this time he kept it leashed. Only his eyes gave him away for they blazed hot with every whimper he drew from her lips, every tremor he coaxed from her body.

She wove her hands in his hair and lost herself to sensation when his lips followed his hands to her breast and he sucked gently. Her nipples peaked for him and she arched against him, wanting more, craving more, but he wouldn't be rushed. He took his time, with long, slow strokes of his hands and with hot, open-mouthed kisses down her body; he took the time to know her.

'Tristan—' She was trembling with the effort of holding her body in check. 'Tristan, please—'

'You want me to be more gentle?'

'No!' She didn't know what she wanted. The passionate intensity he brought to his lovemaking could shoot her so high so fast she could hardly breathe. She'd thought to avoid that this time, she'd thought she wanted tenderness, but his tenderness was destroying her. 'Yes,' she whispered brokenly. She wanted it all.

She opened for him and finally, he moved lower and took her with his tongue. She tried to hold back, heaven help her she did, but within moments she was convulsing around him. Too fast, all of it. The speed with which he'd captured her heart and the road they were travelling on, but she couldn't slow down, not with this man. He was everything she'd ever wanted. Everything she'd never wanted. And she would give him anything he asked.

He waited until her body was limp and her breathing had steadied before kissing his way back up her body. She smelled like sunshine, tasted like sin as he set his lips to her heart and felt it thundering beneath his lips. He moved over her, into her, and the soft, slick slide of his body in hers was almost his undoing. She kissed him then. Put her hand to his cheek and her lips to his and kissed him with emotion so pure it made him tremble. He moved against her, inside her, in a dance he knew would send him soaring.

She was in his head, in his heart, and right now, right now, she was in his arms. His to hold.

And his to love.

CHAPTER TEN

WHEN Erin woke the next morning she was in Tristan's arms and it felt like heaven. She lay there, perfectly still, watching the steady rise and fall of his chest. He was still asleep. It had been late before he'd finally surrendered to sleep. Late, or early, depending on what one called the wee hours of the morning, but when he *had* slept he'd done so dreamlessly. She knew because she'd been watching him, watching over him. Not all the time, she'd caught her own sleep in snatches. But enough.

He wouldn't have wanted that. He'd hate the very thought of it.

She wasn't about to tell him.

She came up on one elbow and eased slowly away from him, trying not to wake him, and found herself caught instead in paying attention to his face in a way that she'd never allowed herself to do when he was awake, not even when they'd been making love. Beautifully male, he was that, with a mouth that spoke of passion tempered by restraint and it mirrored the man exactly. Strength tempered by compassion, sternness softened by humour. A beautiful, unfathomable contradiction.

She didn't know what she would find this morning when he woke. Not yesterday morning's awkwardness, they were past that, or at least she prayed they were. Retreat was more likely; she doubted he was past that. He didn't trust easily. He didn't love easily either.

When he finally did fall in love, she thought wistfully, he would love hard.

She was in the bathroom, filling the kettle with tap water, when he found her. She looked up, startled by the hand that snaked around her waist, and then he was drawing her back against him and locking eyes with her in the mirror. His hair was tousled, boyish, and his eyes, as always, were intent, but it was his tentative smile that commanded her attention.

Lord but it was sweet.

'Breakfast,' she said gravely, 'should be about celebration.'

'You mean food,' he said.

'I mean a gluttonous abundance of food crammed onto trays in the middle of a warm bed with me on one side and a man who makes love like the devil and smiles like an angel on the other. But I'll take three out of four.'

'You think food will be scarce?' His smiles came easily this morning and she delighted in them. 'What if we ordered everything on the menu?'

'Yeah, but what are *you* going to eat?'

His smile grew lazy as his lips brushed her ear. 'Guess.'

Her eyelashes fluttered closed and her breathing grew short. 'Tell you what,' she said. 'You order while I shower and maybe I'll share.'

'You're very generous,' he said as he trailed his hands across her stomach. 'There's just one problem.'

'You think we're going to get crumbs in the bed?'

'No.'

'Spill our drinks?'

'No, although I can see how that would be a problem.'

"What, then?'

'You don't really think you're getting into that shower all by yourself, do you?'

They ordered breakfast once they were clean, and it was double servings all round of scrambled eggs and bacon on Turkish bread, with freshly squeezed orange juice to finish. They were in Branxton, less than two hours from Sydney, and would be home—if they had a mind to be—by lunchtime.

'There's something we need to do before we get back to Sydney,' he said. 'Otherwise it's going to haunt me for all eternity.'

'Really?' This sounded interesting. They'd already managed a fair few things that were going to haunt her for eternity. Hot pools at sunset. Morning showers with Tristan… 'What do we need to do?' He was sitting on the bed opposite her wearing nothing but grey cargo trousers and he was relaxed and easy and there was a teasing glint in his eyes that was irresistible.

'We need to go and climb something.'

'It's called the Ladder of Gloom,' said Erin some two hours later as they stared up at a twelve-metre-high rock face situated on the edge of Kuringai National Park, just north of Sydney. 'It's a lovely, fingery, sports climb and just about perfect for our purposes. Not too high, not too easy, and lots and lots of fun.'

Tristan looked up at the vertical cliff face, at the bulges in the rock, and sighed. 'Who suggested this idiocy?'

'You did. And when you get to the top you'll know why.'

She showed him how to harness up, and went over the equipment with him with relaxed efficiency, explaining as she went. Then she drew him back from the bottom of the cliff face and pointed out their route.

'The first bit's the hardest. If you can climb the first two metres you can climb the rest, so here's what we're going to do. I'll spot you from below to start with, then come up past you and take lead. It's just like climbing a ladder.'

'Although gloomier.'

'Don't worry if you slip. Everyone slips. We'll be roped into ringbolts all the way up.'

'You really like this, don't you?' he asked.

'I really do.'

'You're an adrenaline junkie.'

'I am not!' And with a toss of her head, 'I'm really very sedate when you get to know me. Ask anyone in my family.'

'Not sure that's necessary,' he said dryly. 'Erin, you're not sedate. You move fast, think fast, and make love…fast. Even when you're going slow.'

'Was that a complaint?'

'Hell, no,' he said with a grin. 'That was a compliment.'

Erin's eyes narrowed.

'You'd probably have to be male to understand the depth of that particular compliment,' he said sagely. 'If you'd rather a different compliment I'll keep thinking.' He was, after all, just about to follow her up a twelve-metre vertical rock wall that bulged alarmingly towards the top.

'I'd rather a different compliment,' she said. 'Maybe a sonnet.'

A *sonnet*? Not in this lifetime. 'I might be able to manage a limerick,' he said. 'I'll think about it on the way up.'

Up.

The first two metres were what Erin called skinny. Tristan's interpretation was somewhat more colourful. Five-mil-deep handholds that were nothing but cracks in a rock weren't exactly his idea of a ladder, but up he went. And after Erin had swung past him, bright-eyed and sure-footed, he went up some more. Erin was right. It wasn't a big climb. Twelve metres wasn't that high, but it was strenuous enough to bring a sheen of sweat to his body, and different enough to have him wondering how a climber's arms and hands held up on longer, more difficult climbs.

He was over halfway up before it occurred to him that he, who rarely trusted anyone, had trusted Erin to take the lead. She had the skills. He didn't. That part was logical. That he'd willingly handed over responsibility for their safety wasn't so logical.

He always took point position in the course of his work. He always moved to protect. And here he was, clinging to a cliff face, and if Erin slipped, if she fell, there wasn't a thing he could do about it. He didn't like it. *He* was safe. He was roped in all the way. But she wasn't. Not until she reached each consecutive ringbolt.

'What stops *you* from falling?' he said grimly as she prepared to climb to the next ringbolt.

'Ah,' she said, shooting him a quick smile. 'The mountain strikes its first blow. I wondered if it would. I probably forgot to mention that climbing's all about trust. Trusting yourself, trusting your equipment, and trusting your lead man, or woman, to get you to the top.'

'Don't turn this into a gender argument. It's not.'

'No.' Her gaze was oddly sympathetic. 'In your case it's probably not. It's that overdeveloped protective instinct that's giving you trouble, isn't it? You can't protect me from there and that bothers you.'

'You're vulnerable,' he snapped. And he hated it.

'It's just a little climb,' she said. 'I'll be fine.'

Tristan scowled.

'Apart from that, what do you think?' she asked him as she reached for the next handhold. 'Do you like it? What if you were leading? Would you like it then?'

'Yeah.' Then he would like it. 'Be careful.'

'I'm always careful,' she said, stifling a grin at the glare he sent her. If he'd just relax a little he'd have a much better time of it. He was climbing well for someone who'd not climbed before. His movements were sure; he had no fear of heights. He was strong and agile and he would climb the ladder all the way to the top. She had every confidence in him. He just needed to have the same confidence in her. And that, she realised belatedly, was asking a lot of him. 'We don't have to keep going,' she said, trying to gauge his feelings, but she couldn't read him. He was doing the 'inscrutable cop' thing and doing it well. 'If you're not comfortable the best thing to do is go back down.'

'I'm comfortable enough,' he said gruffly. 'Just don't fall.'

'It's not part of the plan.' She wasn't a reckless climber, but she wouldn't deal in absolutes halfway up a crag. Climbing was a dangerous sport. A challenging sport. Most serious climbers had a tumble or two under their harness. She'd taken a few tumbles herself although now clearly wasn't the time to mention it. She sent him a reassuring smile before turning away to focus on the next leg of the climb, a textbook shimmy up to the next ringbolt.

She made fast work of it and then it was Tristan's turn. He was strong, leanly muscled and in perfect control of his body. 'Beautiful,' she said when he was beside her once more. 'You're a pleasure to watch. That was a compliment, by the way. Just in case you've forgotten what they sound like.'

'Don't you have places to go?' he muttered. 'People to see?'

'I do,' she said. 'I'm going up to the top. And I will see you there.'

The last leg of the climb was Erin's favourite. She liked the bulge in the rock, liked the exhilaration that came with approaching the top of a crag, no matter how high or difficult the climb. She just plain liked getting there. The final move was a scrabbly toe-in and a full stretch to reach the top. She made sure that top hold was secure, that she hadn't grabbed a handful of loose ground, and drew herself up. Her hold was secure, no problem there.

But she was eyeball to eyeball with a brown snake.

Its body was coiled; its head was raised. It didn't look happy. And it wasn't backing down.

She reacted instinctively, snatching her hand away, jerking away, wanting to get out of striking range. She lost her balance, lost her grip, and that was the end of coming back down gracefully.

She wouldn't fall far, she was secured to the lower ringbolt, but she'd hit the wall hard. Better than a brown snake bite though. Much, much better.

He saw her reach the top of the climb. Saw her jerk away from the edge as if stung. He saw her let go and his world stopped. The rock beneath his fingers was hard and unforgiving, his hold on it not nearly deep enough as he reached for her with one hand, reached out to break her fall. He felt his hand brush her shirt, brush her body, but there was nothing to grasp, nothing to clasp. He couldn't stop her. She was tumbling straight past him. And then she reached out to him and he grabbed her and held on tight.

She was falling, falling awkwardly, and it felt as if everything were happening in slow motion. She flung her hand out, looking for purchase and finding nothing, and then Tristan had hold of her, hand to forearm, in a grip that was punishing. She hit the wall, shoulder first but not hard, not nearly as hard as she'd expected to. Tristan had her. Held her.

'Brown snake,' she said, when her heart stopped trying to choke her and she had the breath for speaking. 'At the top.' She looked up at Tristan, at his position. He wasn't secure. She looked at the wall, looked for a handhold or foothold, but there was none. They were all further down. 'Let me go,' she said. 'I won't fall far. Just a couple more metres. I'll pick up a hold further down and come back up.'

'No.' His muscles screamed in protest, and his hold on the rock was perilous, but he would not let her go. It was unthinkable.

'It's okay.' Her eyes were huge. She was dangling in midair, ten metres off the ground, and damned if she wasn't trying to reassure him. 'The rope will stop me. I won't fall far.'

'No.' He would not lose her. Could not. 'Climb.'

So she climbed, using him as her anchor, and when she was secured to the rock beside him and he'd finally released his grip on her arm, she cursed him. 'What was that?' she demanded. 'Have you no concern for your own safety whatsoever? You should have let me go! You could have dislocated your shoulder! What on earth were you thinking?'

'Shut up!' His breathing was ragged, his face was white beneath his tan, and his eyes blazed with a temper that was raging. 'Just shut up. Don't you dare tell me I should have let you go! Do you have *any* idea what watching you fall from the top of that damned rock was *like*?'

That he had a temper was no surprise. That he was letting it rip on the side of a mountain was. She'd scared him, she realised. He hadn't known that her fall would be broken and that she'd be banged up but otherwise fine. He'd only seen her fall. 'I'm fine.' She was starting to tremble. Reaction was setting in. She needed to get to the top before it got the better of her and turned her muscles to mush. 'Tristan, we need to get to the top. Now.'

'What about the snake?' He was calming down. Starting to think ahead, which was good. She needed him calm. She needed him climbing. They needed to get to the top.

'I'll flick some rope up. Scare it away.'

'Why not go down?'

'We can't rap from here. The top's closer. Safer.' Apart from the brown snake and she was going to make damn sure it wasn't waiting for her this time. She was going to bomb that piece of dirt with enough rope and climbing hardware to persuade an elephant to move. 'I'm going up,' she told him. 'Before my muscles give out.' He didn't look convinced. 'Trust me. Please.'

'Are you hurt?' he said gruffly.

'No.' Yes. Her shoulder wasn't in good shape but she could still hold, and if she could hold she could climb. 'We'll check for injuries at the top. You and me both.' And up she went.

She reached the top, bombed that piece of dirt above her with unladylike zeal, and finally, finally hauled over the edge. The snake was gone. She tied off on the double ringbolt at the top and called for Tristan to start climbing.

He came up fast. He'd make a damn fine climber if he had a mind to. Not that he seemed to have a mind to, judging by the rigid set of his jaw and the stern set of his mouth. His introduction to the sport had left a lot to be desired.

She let him settle while she drew up the rope and collected her scattered hardware. When that was done and he still hadn't said a word she sat down a little distance away from him and set about examining the damage.

She'd scraped her leg, a series of long thin gouges that stung like the devil, but they weren't bleeding much. It was her shoulder she was worried about. It was banged up plenty from where she'd rammed into the wall. She rotated it gingerly. She still had full movement; it wasn't dislocated. She felt around her collar-bone, worked her way over her shoulder and upper arm. Nothing *felt* broken.

'You need ice,' he said gruffly.

'Maybe when we get back to the suburbs we can stop by a petrol station.'

'Or a hospital.'

'It's not that bad.' She thought she saw a flash of temper in those glorious golden eyes, but then his jaw tightened and he looked away and the moment was gone.

'It's your call,' he said.

She felt it then. The loss of his protection, the loss of him, clear through to her soul.

The view was superb. The snake was gone. And so was Tristan. He'd retreated deep inside himself. Not shock. She knew the symptoms of shock and he didn't have them. His eyes were clear; he was in control. But he wasn't with her the way he'd been before they'd started to climb. 'I wouldn't have fallen far,' she said, desperately trying to reach him. 'Our second position was still secure. You were still secure.' He looked at her, looked away as if she hurt his eyes. 'Tristan?'

He didn't answer.

'Thank you for catching me.'

'It was instinct.' He still wouldn't look at her. 'I'm sorry if you'd rather I let you fall.'

'No,' she said. 'No. It was better that you caught me, of course it was. I was just scared for you, that's all. We were scared for each other.' She reached out and put her hand on his forearm and he flinched as if struck. 'What is it?' And with a sinking feeling, 'You've hurt your arm.'

'The arm's fine.'

'What, then?'

'It's nothing.' He stood. 'We should head back down.'

'Yes. Yes, we should.' She couldn't get through to him. Not this time. The walls he'd built around himself were too strong. She would try again when they reached the bottom. Maybe once they were off the crag he'd come back from wherever he was. Yes, maybe then he'd be all right.

They rappelled back down to the base of the wall without incident. They packed the climbing gear back into the two packs it had come out of, Tristan covering her hand with his when she reached down to pick one up to carry it to the car. He didn't say a word. He didn't have to. He hefted one pack over his shoulders, held the other like a carryall and started for the car. Erin walked beside him carrying nothing.

'So, I'll drop you at your place, shall I?' she said, when they reached the car, desperately striving for some semblance of normalcy.

'You can't drive with that shoulder,' he said, and opened the passenger door for her. 'I'll drive.'

He was probably right, she thought as she sat in the passenger seat. Her shoulder was really starting to throb and sagging back into the car seat and keeping it motionless felt like heaven. She reached for the seat belt, wincing as she did so, but his hands were already there.

'I'll do it,' he said gruffly, his hands gentle as he drew the seat belt across her body and clicked it into place.

He was so close, so careful of her that she reached out to him again, brushing her fingers against his cheek, and for a moment she thought he would respond. His hand covered hers and he seemed to turn into her caress, but then he was pulling her hand away and placing it gently in her lap. 'Tristan, what is it? What's wrong?'

'We'll go to your mother's,' he said, ignoring her question as he moved away and headed for the driver's seat. 'Patch you up there. You're going to need rest. Looking after.'

'Okay.' She leaned back against the seat and closed her eyes, willing away the tears. Her shoulder hurt, and the scratches on her leg were stinging, but they were nothing compared to the pain in her heart.

She couldn't reach him.

They stopped for ice for her shoulder at the first petrol station they came to and Erin was glad of it. It must have shown on her face because Tristan's eyes grew dark with concern. 'We're going to the hospital,' he said. 'Now.'

She didn't protest.

He drove like a demon to get there. Waited with her in silence, tension radiating from him in waves until her name was called. He walked with her to the door of the examination room, and the look he gave the young intern would have fried a lesser man.

'Take care of her.'

'That's the plan,' said the younger man dryly, and to Erin, 'Come on in and we'll take a look at that shoulder.'

The shoulder was fine, the intern told her when her X-rays came back some half an hour later. She'd torn some muscle and she'd have severe bruising and stiffness, but otherwise she'd be fine. He gave her some painkillers, strapped her shoulder, and ushered her from the cubicle.

Tristan had been sitting, waiting. He stood abruptly when she came out, his focus absolute as he searched her face. He didn't say anything when she approached. He didn't have to. His eyes spoke for him and they gave her hope. He cared for her. Maybe he didn't want to, but he did. It was there in those bruised and shadow filled eyes. She wasn't the only one who'd been beat up by that mountain. Tristan had taken a hammering too.

'The shoulder's going to be fine,' she said gently. 'I've torn a few muscles and bruised the rest, that's all.'

'Best to be sure,' he muttered, shoving his hands in his pockets.

'Yes.' Her smile was gentle too. 'Let's get out of here.'

She gave him directions to her mother's house as they drew closer to it and he followed them in silence. He was silent when they pulled into her mother's driveway as well. Big surprise.

'Here we are,' she said. It was inane but it was the best she could do.

'Head on in,' he said. 'I'll bring your gear in and call for a taxi.'

'Take this car,' she said. 'I can call round for it tomorrow.'

'No.' He shook his head. 'I'll take a taxi.' He gathered up her things and followed her into the house, greeting her mother with a politeness that was as sweet as it was awkward.

'What happened to your shoulder?' asked her mother.

'We went climbing this morning. I gave it a nudge.'

'How big a nudge?'

'Not that big. Nothing's broken. We stopped by the hospital on the way home. Everything's fine. I'm fine.'

'You don't look fine,' said Tristan.

'He's right,' said her mother.

Two against one. 'Honestly, I'm fine. I just need to sit and rest for a bit, that's all.'

'I'll call for that taxi and let you,' said Tristan.

'*I'll* call for the taxi,' she said. 'I can have one here in less than two minutes. I have connections.'

He smiled at that, just a little. 'I'll wait for it outside.' He nodded to her mother, nodded to *her* as if they were nothing but casual acquaintances and headed up the hall. He almost broke her heart.

He felt something for her; she knew that. But whatever it was, it wasn't enough. He was pulling back. Had pulled back. And nothing she said or did seemed to make any difference.

Lillian Sinclair wasn't slow on the uptake. She gave Erin a quizzical look and inclined her head in Tristan's direction as he headed up the hallway. '*I'll* call for the taxi.' Follow him, her look said. Taking a deep breath, Erin did.

She stood back as he unloaded his carryall from the boot and set it at his feet. 'It's over, isn't it?' she said in a small voice. 'Whatever we had, it's over.'

'I don't know,' he muttered. 'Erin, I need time. I need some space. I can't think when I'm near you. You spin me round. You shake things loose that shouldn't be.'

'I don't mean to.'

'I know,' he said. 'I know you don't. I'll call you. In a few days.'

'Really?' She sounded desperate. Men hated that. *She* hated it. 'Well, you know. If you ever need a taxi…'

'Erin, don't,' he said quietly, and she blinked rapidly and looked away.

She couldn't look at him. If she looked at him she was going to cry. 'There's your ride.' She watched him walk up the driveway. She refused to watch him get in the taxi and leave. With a small wave she turned and headed back into the house.

Her mother was waiting for her in the kitchen with the kettle on and coffee beans grinding in the grinder. 'Well?' she asked. 'Did you get the stones you wanted?'

Erin nodded and tried to smile. It didn't work. 'Oh, Mama, I'm such an idiot,' she said. And burst into tears.

CHAPTER ELEVEN

TRISTAN'S Ford arrived at his father's house two days later on the back of a truck that was almost as old as the Ford itself. Frank was driving it. 'How about putting her over to one side of the garage, underneath that elm tree?' said Frank. 'It'll look quite the picture.'

Yeah, thought Tristan. The colour of the rust was a near perfect match for the colour of the falling leaves. He could sweep them into a heap around the old jalopy and no one, his father included, would ever know it was there. 'Good idea,' he said and set about helping Frank unload it. 'You heading back to Lightning Ridge straight away?'

'Nope. I'm gonna get me some culture. I'm booked into a downtown hotel and tonight I'm off to the Opera House to hear Beethoven's piano sonatas numbers one, three, and fourteen.'

'You're a Beethoven fan?'

'Isn't everyone?'

'No.'

'Erin is,' said Frank, nodding his head for good measure. 'That girl knows her classics. How'd she go finding more opal?'

'Nothing caught her eye.'

'Ha!' cackled Frank. 'She knows what she wants; I'll give her that. She caught you yet?'

Tristan gaped at the sun battered older man with his baggy town clothes that hung loosely on his once powerful frame. Age had caught up with Frank's body but it certainly hadn't withered his mind. He was sharp. He saw too much.

'Guess not,' said Frank. 'Pity, 'cause I brought those black opals along, in case you were in the market so to speak. She's a firecracker all right. Just like my Janie. Best twenty years of my life, married to that woman.'

'What happened to your Janie?' asked Tristan.

'She up and died on me. Her heart gave out. I nearly died right along with her.' Frank's face creased into a bittersweet smile. 'Life doesn't come with guarantees, boy, and neither does love. When you find it you hold to it. All you can do. For as long as you can.'

'Wouldn't you rather not have found it at all?'

'Hell, no. A man starts thinking like that and he's only half alive.' Frank eyed him shrewdly. 'You alive, boy?'

'I guess I am.' He eyed Frank right back. 'But I'm still not looking at any black opal. If I was thinking of asking someone to marry me—and I'm not saying I am—I'd take diamonds along for backup.'

'If you're thinking of Erin—and I'm not saying you are—you'd best be looking at the Kimberley Argyles. I've heard her talk about them. She had that look women get in their eyes. You know the one.'

Tristan sighed heavily. He was trying not to think of Erin at all. Problem was he couldn't help it. 'I'd need a fistful of them.'

'Oh, ho!' Frank cackled some more. 'You blew it, didn't you?'

'Big time.' Tristan shoved a couple of bricks behind the wheels of the old car to stop it from going anywhere, not that it seemed to want to. 'I need to call her but I don't know what to say. I don't know where to start.'

'I don't normally give advice without a beer in my hand,' said Frank, 'but for you I'll make an exception. Start with an apology.'

It sounded like good advice. He could use some more of it. 'There's beer in the fridge,' he said. 'Lots of beer. How long before your show?'

The following morning Tristan set about pulling the Ford engine apart. He hadn't called Erin. Not…yet. He would, though. Soon. Just as soon as he was clear on what he was going to say.

Frank was right; it would start with an apology. Yes, it would start with that. The next step was to explain why he'd backed off so fast on the top of that damned cliff and *there* was the rub. The thought of losing her had terrified him. Still terrified him. But walking away from her was impossible, so he was going to have to park his fear somewhere and walk away from *it*. He had to tell her that. He had to open up and talk about his feelings out loud.

He'd do it. He would. Soon.

Just as soon as he got this motor apart and built up the courage for it.

Two hours later he was still no closer to calling her. His shirt was off, his jeans were filthy, and so was just about everything else he'd touched. He wanted to keep the innards of the engine halfway clean but it just wasn't happening. He was swearing like a trooper, and Pat—who'd screeched at him from her cage on the fence line until he'd let her come over—was with him every step of the way, perched on the edge of the Ford's front grille, watching him work while she extended her vocabulary.

'I'm a moron,' he muttered.

'Moron,' said Pat.

'A fool.'

'Fool,' said Pat.

'And how I ever figured you for anything other than female I'll never know,' he said, eyeing the bird darkly. 'Spanner.'

Pat passed him a screwdriver with her claw.

He put it down, picked up the spanner. 'Spanner, Pat. Spanner. *This* is a spanner.'

'Moron,' said the bird.

'She's too impetuous for starters,' he said. 'Asking a complete stranger to go gem-hunting with her for a week. How sensible is that?' Pat handed him another spanner. 'Thank you. She's fearless, Pat. She gives too much. Have you any idea what that does to a man?' Pat handed him a bolt. Tristan had no idea where it had come from. 'Thank you.' He sighed heavily. 'She doesn't want a burnt-out cop in her life. Who would?'

Finally a reason for not calling her that actually made sense.

Until he remembered her innate understanding of the pressure that came with his work. She didn't deal in platitudes, she understood impossible situations and difficult choices and she knew full well they weren't easy to live with afterwards. Sometimes the system asked too much, she'd told him passionately, and he'd known it for truth. She saw into the heart of things. She'd seen into the heart of *him* and she hadn't seen failure. She'd given him strength when he'd needed it, and in return he'd surrendered his heart.

'I'm in love with her, Pat. All the way in love.' There, he'd said it.

Now what?

'I'm putting in for a transfer back to Australia. I'm here to stay.' He still needed to find a place of his own. He still needed to *get* the transfer. But distance was one obstacle he could remove.

'And no more undercover work either. I'm taking a desk job.' He was tired of working undercover. He didn't want to deal in secrets any more. He wanted to be up front about his work. He wanted the people he dealt with to know what he was and what he did. 'From now on I'm living a balanced life.' He needed to be able to offer it to the woman he loved.

'Hobbies.' He punctuated the word with a wave of his spanner.

'Sport.' Another wave of the spanner.

'Hell, Pat, I might even get a pet.' He was on a roll, dreaming big.

'Children.'

Whoa! Children. Where had *that* come from? Perhaps he'd better put the spanner down.

He needed to call Erin. He needed to call her *now*. He

held out the bolt Pat had given him earlier. 'Where did you get this?'

Pat bit him.

'He hasn't called.' Erin was sitting at the counter in her mother's kitchen eating lemon meringue pie, heavy on the double cream, and watching her mother paint an illustration for a children's book of verse. Today's picture was the dark, dark house. The gloomy menace of the dark, dark house suited Erin's mood to perfection. Being in love was difficult enough. Being in love with a soul-wounded, work-weary, overprotective and uncommunicative Interpol cop who hadn't called her in three days was murder. 'He's not going to call.' Her mother dabbed her paintbrush in the grey and started to darken the sky. More menace. Excellent.

'Why don't you call him?' said her mother.

'No.' Erin shook her head vigorously. No. 'My falling down that damned rock face brought everything to a head but he'd have backed off anyway.' She dug her spoon into her piece of pie with a vengeance. 'At the end of the trip or even just before he went back to London. Sooner or later he'd have pulled back. The fall just made him do it sooner, that's all. He doesn't want to love me. He doesn't want to love anyone.'

'You've never known loss,' said her mother. 'You've never known the death of someone who's a part of you. Tristan does. My guess is that when he does love he does it passionately, deeply, and for ever.'

'Go on,' said Erin. 'Rub it in.'

'You made him care for you. And then you took him

up that crag and, in falling, made him face his greatest fear. He thought he'd lost you. And he couldn't handle it.'

'You need more black in the sky,' said Erin. 'God, I'm so depressed.'

'Do you love him?'

'I do.'

'Are you prepared to fight for him?'

'I am. But I'm not calling him. I can't.' She shook her head. 'He has to want to fight for me too.' A phone started ringing. Her phone. The one in her handbag. Her handbag was sitting on the counter. Erin stared at the bag as if it had sprouted fangs, her heart suddenly pounding with equal measures of terror and hope. 'What if it's him?' she whispered.

'What if it's not?' her mother countered dryly.

'What do I do?'

Her mother set her paintbrush on the palette and stared at her with no little amusement. 'Answer it.'

Right. Of course. Yes. First things first. She needed to answer it. She found the phone. Took a deep breath. 'Erin Sinclair.'

'Erin, it's Tristan.'

Erin covered the phone with her hand. 'It's him.'

Her mother rolled her eyes. 'Well, talk to *him*, not *me*.'

Right. Of course. She was about to make a complete fool of herself, nothing surer, so with a wave for her mother she headed out onto the deck. Best she didn't have an audience. 'Hello.'

'I, ah, hope I didn't interrupt anything,' he said.

'No.' No, that didn't sound right. That sounded as if she'd been moping around waiting for him to call.

She needed to sound busier. 'That is, I've been working on my competition pieces this morning, but you didn't interrupt. I was taking a break.' A long one. At her mother's.

'Good,' he said. 'Good. Er, how did the sapphires cut?'

'The tally so far is three shattered practice stones, three shattered big stones and nine that have cut up beautifully. I still have twelve more of the bigger stones and three more practice ones to go.'

'Will you have enough?'

'I'll make it enough.' Excitement crept into her voice. 'Tristan, they're stunning. You should see the colour. It's perfect!'

'I'd like to see them,' he said. 'I'd like to see you. Maybe take you to dinner.'

'You mean like a date?'

She sounded wary, thought Tristan. After the way he'd treated her, she had every right to be. 'Or a movie,' he said quickly. 'Dinner and a movie. Or, we could do something else. We could meet for coffee or go on a picnic.' Whatever she wanted.

'We could go climbing.'

Except that. Tristan raked a hand through his hair and looked to the sky for inspiration. 'We could,' he said carefully. 'We could do that. I might even manage a civil word afterwards. Provided you didn't fall.' If she fell, all bets were off. 'How's the shoulder?'

'Sore. And, to be honest, climbing's out for a while on account of it.'

'Shame.'

'Liar.'

There was laughter in her voice. A warmth that slid straight through him and he relaxed enough to say what was foremost on his mind. 'I hurt you. We got to the top of that rock and I couldn't shake the image of you falling. I wasn't there for you. I couldn't deal with the thought of losing you. I'm sorry.'

'You didn't lose me.' There was no laughter in her voice now. It was so small he could hardly hear it. 'I'm still here.'

He needed to see her face. He desperately needed to see her eyes. 'I'd like to start over,' he said, his heart hammering in his chest. 'I'd like to go slower this time and get it right. I'd like to take you to dinner. '

'I'd like that.' Her voice was slightly stronger now. 'When?'

'Tonight?' No. She only had a couple more weeks to prepare her competition pieces. He didn't want to jeopardise her chances by monopolising her time. 'Any time,' he amended. No, that sounded too casual. 'But tonight would be good.'

'Tonight it is. What time?'

'Seven.' Seven sounded about right. Except that it was five hours away. 'Six. I'll pick you up at six.' He was as nervous as a teenage boy asking a girl out for the very first time. He didn't even know where she lived. 'I'll need your address.'

She gave it to him. And then she hung up.

It was four-thirty when Erin pulled up in Tristan's driveway. She'd started cutting two more sapphires, shattered the third, and decided she needed the rest of the afternoon off. She wasn't sure where they were going for dinner but she'd dressed casually in anticipation of somewhere fairly relaxed. Okay, that was a lie. It had taken her over an hour to decide what to wear and although at first glance her attire could be mistaken for casual, on second glance it was not. Her shirt was a rich and flattering shade of watermelon and clung in all the right places, her skirt was a cool forest-green with a gauzy black undersheath, designer cut to whisper around her calves as she walked, and her shoes, well, they were black and strappy and they weren't made for walking at all. They were made for seduction. She wore half a dozen slim gold bangles at her wrist for music, a watermelon tourmaline pendant at her neck for luck. She was ready for anything.

She saw Frank's old Ford, Tristan's Ford now, off to one side of the garage. The bonnet was up. And then she saw Tristan.

One look at him in his torn work jeans, with his hair tousled and his muscled torso gleaming in the sunlight, and she damn near forgot her own name, let alone what she was wearing. He flashed her a smile and reached for what she thought was a rag, but it wasn't a rag, it was a T-shirt and he was dragging it over his head and down across his body.

Okay, so he hadn't known she was coming over early. He'd still heard her pull into his driveway, hadn't he? She'd driven the Monaro; he'd have to be deaf not to. He could have covered up before she'd stopped the car and started looking for him, but no. He'd waited until she'd seen him without it and *then* put his shirt on.

He was torturing her deliberately.

She took her time getting out of the car, making sure her skirt rode way up and that he had a clear view before leisurely smoothing it back into place. Two could play at that game.

'Afternoon,' he said.

'Isn't it. Afternoon, Pat.'

Pat moved along the edge of the car, closer to Tristan, and fixed her with a beady eye. Protective.

'I cut three stones and got the fidgets so I came on over. I'm interrupting, aren't I? You're busy… bonding.' She eyeballed Pat right back. 'You *do* realise that bird is in love with you?' Tristan looked at Pat. Pat moved closer. The look on Tristan's face was priceless. 'Guess not.'

Tristan had never seen anything more beautiful than Erin Sinclair, dressed to stop a man's heart. That she knew she could stop it didn't lessen her appeal one little bit. The only thing stopping him from dragging her into his arms there and then was the small matter of him being covered in dirt and grease and smelling like a farm animal. 'I need a shower.' He put a protesting Pat back in her cage and all but ran for the kitchen. He pulled a beer from the fridge, cracked it open, and handed it to Erin. 'I'll be right back.'

'Handsome, you just take your time. I'm not going anywhere.' Her smile was Gidget but her words were pure Mae West.

He managed to saunter down the hallway, at least until he was out of sight.

He hit the shower at a dead run.

By the time he made it back to the kitchen, showered, shaved, and dressed for dinner, he'd calmed down somewhat. Until she went to the fridge, pulled a beer from it, cracked the top, and handed it to him. The beer went on the counter and his arms snaked around her. She came willingly, eagerly, as her lips met his for a kiss that was staggeringly potent. He let her go almost as abruptly as he'd reached for her. He wanted to do this right this time. He wanted to take his time.

He didn't have a chance in hell.

'Dinner,' he muttered. 'We're going out to dinner. Now.'

He took her down to Circular Quay and they chose a busy seafood restaurant that overlooked the Quay and the Opera House. It was lively and casual as opposed to intimate and romantic. He was almost certain he could keep his hands off her for the duration of the meal.

'I love this place,' she said as she browsed the menu. 'I never know what to order. I want it all.'

'What about the seafood platter?'

Her eyes grew dreamy.

He ordered the platter and a bottle of white to go with it. 'How are your competition pieces coming along?' he said, and she seemed to come back down to earth with a thud.

'I hadn't counted on having so many sapphires, or having to cut them myself,' she said with a worried frown. 'I figure if I work day and night for the next two weeks I might just get everything I want to get done, done.'

'Are you driving taxis next week?'

'Three shifts.'

'Can you get someone else to drive them?'

'Yes, but there's this small matter of rent.'

'There's also the small matter of your future. You need to prioritise.'

'I am. I will.'

'I'll cover your rent for a couple of weeks.'

'You will not!' Her eyes flashed fire. 'But thank you for offering.'

She was as hard to help as his sister, he decided glumly. Women. 'Okay, here's the plan. It supersedes my original plan, which was to take you to bed and keep you there for the next twenty years or so.'

'What about your job?' she said. 'You know, the one in *London*?'

'I'm putting in for a transfer to Sydney.'

'Oh.' She seemed taken aback. 'Well, why didn't you say so?'

'I did. Just then. Do you want to hear the new plan or not?'

Her smile was slow in coming but when it did it damn near fried what was left of his brain. 'I'm all ears.'

'The new plan,' he said doggedly, 'involves taking you home at the end of the evening and staying away from you until your competition pieces are done.'

Erin sighed heavily. 'I liked your original plan better.' She picked up her wineglass, toyed with it. 'Are you really putting in for a transfer to Sydney?'

'Cops' honour.'

They were back at his place by eleven. He didn't ask her in. Instead, he leaned down and brushed his lips against hers in the briefest of kisses. She had a rainbow to chase. And he had to keep that in mind.

'What was that?' she said indignantly. 'Because whatever it was it wasn't nearly enough.'

His smile was slow in coming and he hoped it fried her brain. 'That was goodnight.'

Strawberries arrived from Tristan at breakfast the following morning. The day after that it was bodysurfing with him at Bondi Beach at dawn. He took her home after that. Took her home so she could work.

The days passed slowly. Erin drove taxis and worked on her pieces. Tristan tracked down car parts and worked on his Ford. His Holden arrived, he told her on one of his brief visits, and he was pulling that apart too. Pat was helping him.

The weekend arrived and Erin finished the earrings for the competition. Tristan took her fishing from a friend's houseboat on the Hawkesbury to celebrate. They stayed there half the day and he never once looked tempted to move from the fishing deck to the bed inside and make use of it. He was sweet; he was sexy. He was a perfect gentleman.

He caught three fish.

The following afternoon she took him to the Opera in retaliation. Three solid hours of Berlioz. She delighted in the sight of him in a suit almost as much as she delighted in his suffering.

Her need for him grew claws but she didn't give in to it. She took that shimmering sexual tension he could create in her with a glance and poured it into her work.

She finished the bracelet and the brooch, and the daintiest of hairclips.

She finished the necklace with two days to spare.

She slept for an hour, lay in a steaming hot bubble bath for almost as long, and throwing on some clothes and rolling her finished pieces in velvet and tucking them into her handbag, she went in search of an audience.

She found Tristan and Pat—deep in conversation—as they did whatever it was they were doing to the Ford. They made a pretty picture, it was a pretty spot, but it wasn't quite the unveiling location she had in mind. She collected them up and with food, love, and an audience of more than mere man and bird in her sights she headed for Lillian Sinclair's kitchen.

Her mother was painting when they arrived. Erin wasn't the only one working to a deadline. Today's illustration was for 'Tiger, tiger, burning bright'. Erin stared hard at the glowing golden eyes and strong, sinewy lines her mother had created and sighed her approval. 'He's so beautiful,' she said. 'He's so...' Familiar was the word she was looking for. Her gaze slid from the illustration, to Tristan, and then back.

Her mother smiled angelically. 'Wonderful thing, inspiration. You never know where you'll find it next.' She saw Tristan seated at the counter and Pat—in her travelling cage—seated beside him. 'You look well,' she told Tristan, studying him from over the top of her purple-framed glasses. 'You're getting more sleep. And *you*,' she turned her attention to Pat, 'are positively glowing.'

'It's the love of a good man,' murmured Erin, *sotto voce*. 'I should be so lucky.'

'Was there a reason for bringing us here other than to practise your comedy routine?' asked Tristan dryly.

'Indeedy there was.' Erin delved into her bag for her roll of buff-coloured velvet and rolled it out along the counter. When Tristan studied them intently, her mother's expression grew reverent, and even Pat looked at them in silence, Erin knew she'd surpassed herself. Win or lose, she was satisfied with her efforts. Of course, she would prefer to *win*.

'You finished them,' said Tristan slowly.

'So I did.'

'We need champagne,' said her mother and headed for the fridge. Grinning, Erin went in search of champagne flutes. A girl had to love a mother who kept champagne in the fridge, just in case.

'Any news on your transfer?' she asked Tristan, just in case there was more than one reason to celebrate.

'It came through a few days ago.'

Erin paused, midway through opening the champagne. 'And you didn't think it worth mentioning?'

'I was waiting for the opportune moment.'

She narrowed her eyes. 'It's here.'

'I'm not working car theft any more,' he said. 'I'll be tracking down stolen diamonds.'

'Get out of here!'

'Seriously.'

'Is it undercover work?'

'Not for me, although there will be men in the field. I'll be running the show from a desk here in Sydney.'

'It sounds demanding.'

'It will be,' he said, his gaze on hers, intent and searching. 'But it's what I do. Part of who I am.'

'I know that.' She shot him a smile. Maybe they could open the champagne after all. The cork popped and she reached for the flutes. Pat got a grape from the fruit bowl.

'You don't mind?' he said.

'Mind? I think I'm jealous.'

'There'll be travel involved, particularly at the start,' he said, and Erin nodded. He would need to be hands on to begin with; she expected no less of him.

'You like to travel, remember?'

'I do, but I distinctly remember you objecting rather strenuously to the tyranny of distance when it came to relationships. Not to mention secrets. I may not be working undercover but there'll still be things I can't talk about. And there'll still be things I *won't* talk about,' he said quietly. 'I know what you want in a partner, Erin. I know I'm not it.'

Her mother was quiet. Even Pat was quiet. They were all looking at her, but it was Tristan she looked to. Tristan who was laying his life out in front of her, warts and all.

'Yes, well, I'm currently reviewing my criteria with regards to what I want in a partner.' She looked to her mother and sent her a grateful smile for her wisdom and for the example she set. 'I'm thinking that if you find the right man the balance will come.'

'I have to go to the Kimberleys in the morning,' he said gruffly. 'I'll be gone for a few days.'

He still wasn't convinced of her sincerity. But he would be, Erin decided firmly. Eventually. 'If I'm starting to look a little green don't be alarmed. It's just envy.'

'You could come with me.'

Erin groaned. 'It's very, *very* tempting, don't get me wrong. But maybe you should go alone this time. Ask me again when there's less pressure on you to get your operation set up.' He'd encouraged her to focus on her work when she needed to. She could do no less in return.

He smiled at that. 'I'll look around on your behalf. Take notes. Anything in particular you're interested in?'

'The flawless whites. No, the cognacs. No... *The Pinks*.'

'Jezebel,' said Pat.

'Where *does* she get her vocabulary?' said Erin.

'Second book of Kings,' said her mother. "And the dogs shall eat Jezebel in the portion of Jezreel, and there shall be none to bury her." '

'Amen,' said the bird.

'Oh, go eat your grape,' said Erin.

'Don't look at me,' said Tristan. 'Pat and I don't talk religion. I only teach her modern language skills.'

'Moron,' said Pat affectionately. And gave him her grape.

Tristan drove Erin home from Lillian's after dinner and she fell asleep on the way. She'd had a glass or two of champagne over the course of the evening but that wasn't it. She was exhausted. He didn't know how many hours she'd put in on her competition pieces but he suspected it had been enough this past week to bring her to the point of exhaustion. She was still driving taxis. She'd still managed to spend time with *him*. But it had cost her.

'Stay,' she whispered when he picked her up as he would a sleepy child and carried her to the door.

'You need sleep,' he muttered. 'If I stay you won't get it.'

'Stay anyway.'

'What is it about timing?' he muttered.

'What's wrong with the timing?' She stifled a yawn. 'The timing's perfect.'

'Just a few more days,' he muttered. '*Then* it'll be perfect.' He set her down, kissed her on the forehead. 'I'll miss you,' he said, and then he was gone.

CHAPTER TWELVE

IT WAS official. Erin Sinclair was not a patient woman. Oh, she *could* have been a patient woman, thought Erin darkly. If Tristan had come to her bed when she'd asked him and spent the night making wild, passionate love to her she could have been positively saintly when it came to waiting for him to return. But he hadn't. And boy was she going to make him pay.

She spent the three days he was away driving taxis and plotting her next step. She submitted her competition pieces and cleaned Rory's car, polishing and detailing it until it gleamed. She adored the easygoing, laid-back Tristan. She looked at him and saw for ever and it was bright with rainbows and sunshine after rain. She looked at him and saw a man who loved hard and loved deeply. She wanted him to love her like that.

He was staying in Sydney, building a life. He seemed to be building one with room for her in it. He was being such a gentleman and she loved that about him. Really. She did.

But if he didn't make love to her soon she was going to explode.

He called her the following morning to tell her he was back. He asked if she was busy and when she said she wasn't he asked her over. It was time to put her plan in motion.

He was sitting on the top step of his father's verandah when she arrived, drinking coffee and looking sexier than any man had a right to look. She pulled into his driveway with a five-point-seven litre V8 rumble and he smiled and shook his head. When she shimmied her way out of the car his smile grew rakish.

She was wearing a little blue dress that was short enough and tight enough to make a man beg.

And he *was* going to beg.

'Welcome back,' she said when she reached him, leaning over to settle a whisper-light kiss on his lips. It didn't stay whisper-light for long. His hand came up to cradle the back of her head, he slanted his lips over hers, and unleashed a deep and urgent passion that left her weak and wanting more.

She ended the kiss with a nip to his lower lip and watched his eyes blaze with no little satisfaction. '*Tiger, tiger, burning bright.*' She was about to pull this one's tail.

She settled down on the step just below him, making sure he had an excellent view of her cleavage. 'There I was this morning,' she said. 'Sitting there staring at the Monaro—as you do—and all of a sudden I had this hankering to see how fast it went.'

Tristan's smile widened. 'You got a speeding ticket, didn't you?'

'Not at all,' she said airily. 'A girl in my line of work can't be going around collecting speeding tickets. I'd be out of a job. No, I phoned an old friend of the family who has a dirt racetrack in western Sydney. It's mine for the day.'

'Your brother's going to kill you.'

'He owes me. I figure this will make us about even.'

Tristan looked at her. Looked at the car. 'No, he's going to kill you.'

'Yes, well, I was wondering if you'd like to join me.'

'To stop him from killing you?'

'He's not here. He's not even in the country. Forget the killing part. Because, seriously, you're way too focussed on death.' This wasn't going according to plan. He was supposed to jump at the chance to put the Monaro through its paces. 'Do you, or do you not, want to come and drive this car at speed around an empty dirt racetrack this morning?'

'It's bait,' he said. 'You're up to something.'

'Cops are so suspicious. I hate that.'

'I'm right, aren't I?'

'I hate that too.'

'I love this car,' said Erin an hour later, pitching her voice above the throaty roar of an engine that was being put through its paces. They were midway round the bottom curve of the figure-eight dirt racetrack and Erin was driving, her hands sure and firm on the wheel. The Monaro's front wheels were currently tracking a tight line around the bend. The rest of the car was following. She handled the car with a confidence born of fearlessness and a hefty dose of devilry.

She was doing it deliberately.

Tristan's nerves were good. He hadn't cracked yet. And then she hit the straight and hit the accelerator. The speedometer hit two-hundred kmph three quarters of the way down the two kilometre straight and Tristan started praying. 'There's a corner coming up,' he said with as much nonchalance as he could muster. 'Just thought I'd mention it.'

She hit the brakes and slid into the corner, taking an outside line this time with spectacular sideways results. He knew cars, knew she was in perfect control of this one, but it didn't seem to make a jot of difference. She was precious to him; he was dying a thousand little deaths, not because of what *was* happening but at the thought of what *could* happen. He wanted her to pull over and park the car. Instead, he attempted to be rational and park his fear instead. He was doing it. He was. And then she spoke.

'I know,' she said, slanting him a naughty pixie smile. 'Let's talk about us.'

'You mean *now*?' He couldn't believe the way a woman's mind worked. 'Wouldn't you rather—oh, I don't know—concentrate on your *driving*?'

'Not at all.' But she didn't accelerate quite as aggressively out of the corner this time. Thank God.

'Are you sure you wouldn't rather talk about this over coffee? Or beer? What about scotch?' he said. 'I know this bar. It's quiet. Private. *Stationary*.' The last word was a roar to match the engine.

'When are we going to make love again?'

That did it. 'Pull over.'

'Pardon?'

She'd heard him, nothing surer, but just in case she hadn't he roared a little louder. 'I was *going* to do this the traditional way. There was going to be moonlight and music, palm trees and a hot pool. Maybe even a horse or two.'

'It's a pretty picture, to be sure,' she said. 'But let's face it. It's been done before.'

'I was *going* to come for you in a meticulously restored thirty-nine Ford, bearing a picnic basket full of food—'

'Presumably some time this decade,' she said. 'When were you going to get around to the lovemaking bit?'

'And propose to you then, but—'

'Propose?'

She hit the brake hard and they came to a sliding, screeching halt amidst a cloud of smoke and dust. 'There go the brake pads.'

'Define *propose*.'

'You know. Ask the woman I love beyond reason to be my wife, but no. You had to rush me. So now you're just going to have to make do.'

She was staring at him with what looked a lot like dismay. It wasn't exactly reassuring. 'I know I'm not what you want,' he continued raggedly. 'I'm overprotective. There'll be details of my work that I can't share with you, won't share with you. But I will always put you first and I will always love you.'

Erin's eyes filled with tears.

'Don't cry,' he said. 'You're not supposed to cry. I'm doing this all wrong, aren't I?'

'No.' Her tears started to fall. 'No, it's perfect.'

He hadn't bought her an engagement ring. He dug

in his pocket for what he had bought for her. 'Hold out your hand.'

Wiping the tears from her eyes, Erin did as she was told. Her hand was trembling, her whole body was trembling, and when he turned her hand palm upwards and poured a fistful of rough diamonds into it she shook even more.

'The big one's the pink,' he said. 'But there's whites and champagnes and cognacs as well. Whatever you don't want for yourself I thought you could use for your business.'

She couldn't see them through her tears but it didn't matter. She would ogle them later. Right now she had more important things to do. 'I love you,' she said fiercely. 'You're all I'll *ever* want and don't you dare think otherwise.' She closed her fist around the diamonds he'd given her, holding them tight. 'Tell me what you want.'

He took a deep, ragged breath. His heart was in his eyes. He was the most beautiful thing she'd ever seen. 'I want you to be my wife. I want laughter, even if it's sometimes mixed with tears. I want a lifetime of it. With you.'

'Yes,' she said.

His smile was the sweetest she'd ever seen. He was going to kiss her now, nothing surer. And then he was going to make wild and passionate love to her, just as she'd planned. She loved it when a plan came together. He looked out the window at the deserted racetrack, looked back at her, and this time his smile was rakish. 'And I'd really, *really* like to drive.'